Joe was try **profile.**

But it was dark, and all he could see were her shining eyes, glittery eyes, beautiful pale blue eyes. Her gaze glued itself to the stage.

She tucked a light curl behind her ear, and that motion struck a chord with him. A strangely familiar chord. Like seeing *the girl next door.*

As he turned to leave, he lifted the program from the seat and, not paying attention, rammed into her back. "I'm sorry. I'm afraid I've been more than a bit of a nuisance tonight."

"Not to worry." Her voice carried over her shoulder, cheerful in spite of all she'd endured at his expense. She'd probably get out and away from him as quickly as possible.

And then she glanced back.

His mouth nearly unhinged. That was why she looked familiar. Victoria Banks. "I guess I'll always be saying I'm sorry to you, won't I?"

Her large eyes widened. "Well, if it isn't Joseph Huntington from Miss Davies's Dance School. The graduation dance. All grown-up." Then her eyes narrowed. "Or is that Sergeant Huntington?"

He groaned. "And I stepped on your foot…again."

Books by Linda S. Glaz

Love Inspired Heartsong Presents

With Eyes of Love
Always, Abby
The Substitute Bride
The Preacher's New Family
Bride by Necessity
The Soldier's Homecoming

LINDA S. GLAZ

is married with three children, all grown, but that gives her so much time to write. She loves soccer and karate, which she taught for more than twenty-five years, and adores theater—especially musicals. She has two novellas and six novels all published or contracted, and has six suspense novels waiting to find homes. She also works as a literary agent for Hartline Literary Agency. Why does she do so much? She has a triple-A personality and must stay busy.

LINDA S. GLAZ

The Soldier's Homecoming

HEARTSONG
PRESENTS

Recycling programs
for this product may
not exist in your area.

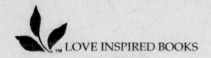 LOVE INSPIRED BOOKS

ISBN-13: 978-0-373-48729-5

The Soldier's Homecoming

Copyright © 2014 by Linda S. Glaz

www.Harlequin.com

Printed in U.S.A.

And we know that all things work together
for good to them that love God, to them
who are the called according to His purpose.
—*Romans* 8:28

To my granddaughter, Victoria, who loves to dance,
and who is a precious light in our lives.
Love you, beautiful!

Chapter 1

Howell, Michigan
June 1945

Victoria Banks spun on her toes until an unexpected wave of dizziness forced her to stop. She grabbed the edge of the wooden counter, but her students circled around clapping for more. She offered one last, unsteady pirouette and then brought class to a halt. "Enough for tonight." Hand over heart, she laughed at the girls' antics.

Like miniature cartoon dancers, her youngest class of ballerinas spun like the tops of music boxes. Round and round until Victoria felt faint. "No more. No more."

"Awww," Suki, a redhead whose curly hair was always in a mess, moped.

The little blonde with eyes more golden than moonbeams said, "C'mon, Ms. Banks. Again. Again."

"Please...."

Wiping perspiration from her face with a towel as her breath came in short gasps, Victoria attempted a smile. "No *more* today. We're finished with this lesson, and I hope you'll all go home and practice. Goodness knows I need some rest from all of you little bundles of energy." Mother had been right, as usual. She shouldn't have stayed out so late with her best friend, Florence, last night. Today she was paying for her foolishness.

She just needed to catch her breath, that was all. During the lessons her girls somehow managed to get her to demonstrate more than she ever planned. But tonight she had to hurry, because tonight she and Flo were catching the train into Lansing to see Phillipe dance *Swan Lake*. Oh, Phillipe Mandrin. Dancer extraordinaire. Not just a wonderful dancer, but a French *danceur*.

Flo's older brother, David, and his wife would meet them at the station and escort them to dinner. From there, they were on their own until three hours later when David would pick them up from the theatre. Then they would spend the night with David and Louisa and ride back with them to Howell the next day. Flo said they were anxious for a visit with the home folks. What a glorious respite from the everyday.

With a wave to her final student, she collapsed in the only comfortable chair in her studio. A lavender pillow stitched by one of her students padded the seat.

She stared at the cover of *En Pointe* magazine, her favorite. All the news about ballet...and more. Did all girls fall in love with celebrities? She supposed so. Flo did. Phillipe Mandrin. Such a handsome, mysterious

Frenchman. And apparently so did she, because Phillipe carried her heart in his palm.

Then she laughed at herself. How foolish to think she was enamored with a man she'd never met, a celebrity. Like believing she was in love with Tigers' pitcher Tommy Bridges when she was fifteen.

As a child she had longed to grow up and play professional baseball, but no one in her family thought it appropriate for a girl. Why not? After all, men danced ballet. Why couldn't girls play ball? Had she realized it then, male dancers would have been fuel for her arguments with her parents. Particularly her father. She giggled remembering what a little monster she'd been as a child.

And now her heart beat faster than a frightened bird's whenever she thought of the deliciously talented Frenchman. Black hair and brown eyes reached from his picture on the magazine covers and stared her in the face. Coming from different worlds, they would never meet, but if only they could. If only... But those things didn't happen, not to girls from Howell, Michigan. After all, Mandrin was famous and every girl in America who loved dance loved Phillipe.

Joseph Huntington stepped from the noisy train platform in the company of a dozen or more other returning soldiers. Glancing through a haze of blue-gray smoke and steam, he noticed most of the soldiers running into outstretched arms. Khaki-green and ruby-red joined together into focus as pretty girls kissed men's hungry lips, and the girls' warm fingers were feverishly snatched and pressed against the men's coat breast pockets. Joe smiled at the happiness surrounding him even though no one waited for his smile, his kiss or his out-stretched and welcoming hand.

Automobile horns blasted and he jumped out of the way. Then a whistle blew, startling him again as he picked up his heavy duffel bag. How long would this jumpiness last? He was no longer under attack. "Pardon me. Excuse me." He staggered against the throng of people, doing his best to avoid running anyone over. Though that gorgeous girl two feet in front of him would be nice to run into. He sighed and skirted around her. "Coming through." He brushed against blue-and-white polka dots and seamed nylons.

The girl stopped and dazzled him with her blinding smile. His heart pounded at the unfulfilled wishes swirling in his mind. He sighed to himself but took another peek.

Oh, well, he'd catch a ride into the heart of the city, get a room, have dinner and then if he finished in time, he'd treat himself to the ballet. Something relaxing, something that showed the better side of humanity. Something that assured him he was truly home. Maybe some—one. With ruby lips and a polka-dotted skirt and seamed nylons who could dance all night.

Joe had always admired folks who could dance, even though he himself had been born with two left feet as evidenced by the feeble attempts he'd made at Ms. Davies's Dance and Etiquette School. "The way to get a girl," his brother, Daniel, had claimed. The way to have a girl hate him was more like it.

Joe frowned as he recalled all the dainty feet he'd tromped on. Scrawny little girls like that feisty Victoria Banks. She was probably filled out and even prettier now. Or playing professional ball. He chuckled. Wasn't that what she'd said she wanted to do just before she stuck her tongue between her lips, wound up her arm and blasted him in the eye with a curve ball? He drew in a sharp breath. Holding a girl in his arms at fifteen was downright painful, but as he looked about at all of the intimate homecomings surrounding him, suddenly it didn't seem that bad an idea. Not even if that meant cozying up to the pitcher of the Walnut Street Sluggers.

The memory was accompanied by a groan. His graduation dance had ended any chance of that. What a disaster.

Victoria had floated around the dance floor, light on her feet and dazzling—nothing like Babe Ruth. All the other guys had wanted her for their date, but Joe had asked first, and she honored his request. Then, after his dance with Dru Carraway, the class wallflower, Dru had become sick. Joe, wanting to be a gentleman, had offered to drive her home. Only he couldn't find Victoria to tell her. Still, Victoria shouldn't have been so angry.

It wasn't as though he'd tried to be a jerk. When he returned to the dance, Victoria was gone. Someone else had driven her home. His buddy Steve said she'd been mad as a badger for his leaving without her.

He'd called no fewer than a dozen times, but Victoria refused his calls. So immature. Just like on the ball diamond when she pegged him in the eye.

Well, that was long ago, long before he'd signed on to fight for Uncle Sam. Now he had to get serious, buckle down and find work. There was no time to worry about past experiences. Bad *or* good.

However, he would treat himself to a night out. Phillipe Mandrin and his partner, Genevieve DuMont, whom he'd heard about while stationed in Germany, would be a onetime luxury until he had his dream job. Meaning any job that brought in money and took him closer to starting his own company. He'd promised himself he wouldn't get sidetracked by a pretty face when the one thing he had worked for was within his grasp.

"Joseph, over here!"

"What?" Joe turned to the sweet melody coming from a beautiful blonde's mouth. But a burly private rushed past him into the waiting arms. What had he expected? No one waited for him, not here, not anywhere. Even his parents were gone.

Before hailing a cab, he reached for his wallet to be sure it still rested in his pocket. He'd saved all his pay to make a fresh start now that the war was over. Returning to Howell to do just that was within his reach. Another train ride after his big night in the city, and he'd find himself at the family home. His folks gone now, he'd have the house to care for. No doubt it needed a lot of upkeep at this point. He sighed. How could he complain? Dan, an attorney with a growing family, had paid the taxes while Joe was away, keeping the property up the best he could. But Joe realized Dan had his own home to care for all this time and he couldn't expect too much.

"You served for both of us, so I was able to stay home with my family. It's the least I can do for you," he'd told Joe in a letter. Well, okay. It was a fair trade and he'd accepted with a heart full of gratitude.

Joe quickly calculated what a couple of cans of paint and some brushes cost.

An old man with a gray halo munching on a thick, soggy cigar slapped him on the back, interrupting his daydreams. "Way to go, young fella. Wish I could have been there with you. But I did my time in the Great War." He shook his head and pulled the cigar from his lips a second time, the blast of smoke lingering. "So many boys killed then. Us doughboys took a few beatings, but we doled out some licks o' our own till we beat 'em good." When he looked back up, a smile loaded with creases replaced his melancholy expression. "Enough of that. Welcome home." And this time, he slugged Joe in the shoulder as if to say *I understand what you've been through, son.* "Glad you made it back all in one piece."

Joe slid his hand forward in a firm grip. "Thank you, sir."

"What? Speak up, young fella."

Joe raised his voice and offered a small salute. "Thank you." His heart squeezed in his chest as he imagined what it must have been like in this man's war. He'd heard stories from the older soldiers. None of them good. Joe noticed the hitch in the man's step as he walked away.

Then he gazed past the heartbreaking memories of the men his platoon had lost, and feeling particularly blessed at the moment, he hailed a cab.

After a glorious train ride followed by dinner with Flo's brother, Victoria and Florence hopped from David's car. They tugged their coats closer and hurried to the opera hall where Mandrin would be performing. In front of the building, Victoria danced a quick step about Flo. "Look. Look at the picture of the two of them dancing. Have you ever seen such a beautiful couple? Lookit, Flo! Oh, he's such a handsome man. An absolute dream in a bottle. If only…"

Flo's lip quivered. "Let's get inside. It's too cold to be staring at a picture." She clutched her coat tighter and planted a hand on her hat to keep it from blowing away. "We can see the real thing inside."

"How can you say that? Look at those eyes. Doesn't he simply melt your heart?" Victoria grabbed Flo's arm and clung to her elbow as they pushed forward toward the window. "I can't wait."

Flo prodded her. "Then let's move inside."

The old ticket taker's eyebrows, like caterpillars on a stem, rose as if she were asking, "Well, do you want tickets or not?"

"Yes, ma'am. Two tickets, please." Victoria's voice trembled. "As close to the stage as you have." She snapped up the tickets and stared at her best friend. "See here? At least they aren't in the nosebleeds." She smiled at the woman in the cage. "I was afraid you might be sold out."

"You girls are lucky. Plenty up top, but we had a cancellation of fifteen right in the middle. You'd better call this your lucky day."

Victoria hoped her smile reflected the appreciation she felt. Not luck, this was a blessing!

The two girls quickly bypassed stragglers and scurried their way to row M, seats 9 and 11. "We're almost in the middle. I can't believe our good fortune. I don't know who our benefactors were, but I'm so glad they canceled at the last minute. I'd have been happy in the top row. Just to see Phillipe dance." Victoria placed a hand to her chest to steady her racing heart. Seeing Phillipe certainly had her in a tizzy.

Flo, her usual calm self, slid into her seat without a word. "Isn't this hall incredible?" She pointed to the overhanging ceiling. "Look at all of the intricate details. The gold leaf, the carvings. Oh, what a treat. Thank you for asking me to come along."

"Why, I'd no more leave my best friend than a piece of chocolate cake."

Flo giggled. She knew Victoria would *never* leave a piece of cake.

The lights came down almost immediately, not giving them any time to read their programs. In the dark, Flo peeked over the top of her program, excitement shining in her eyes. "Thank goodness we arrived in time. They're starting already. And it's such poor manners to arrive late."

Nodding, Victoria tugged the pin from her hat, pressed it back into the felt and then set her hat carefully on her lap so as not to smudge it. After all, she didn't buy a new hat every day what with fabric so dear during the war; a new article of clothing meant more than usual.

"Excuse me. Pardon me." A deep voice cut through the darkness along with a giant of a man. "So sorry," the man whispered loud enough for everyone to hear. "I beg your pardon."

"Ouch!" The big lug. "Shh." And where were *his* manners? Flo was right; people could be so rude. Victoria spied army drab passing to her right. A soldier. Her heart softened. She could be a bit more forgiving. Her hat slid from her lap, but when she reached for the brim, warm hands grabbed it as it hit the floor.

"Excuse me." Okay, so he had manners after all. "Terribly sorry. I didn't mean to step on your foot." He held the scuffed hat aloft. "And now this. Please, forgive me for being such an oaf. And such a beautiful hat. Is your foot all right?"

"Certainly," she whispered. "You walked on the top and I walk on the bottoms." It was the expression her father used to put someone at ease whenever his foot was inadvertently stepped on.

Her father had a gentleness about him, an extra special kindness. Except when she was young and wanted to grow up to play ball. He hadn't tried to be gentle on that account. She huffed at the vivid memory.

Her plans for her thirteenth birthday had been for a party to remember. It was memorable, all right. Had it really been ten years ago already since he'd made it his business to put his foot down and have his own way?

Victoria thought back to the present her parents had given that year. The monstrosity took up the entire corner of her bedroom.

"What is it again, Mom?" Her face twisted into a knot in spite of her efforts to appear polite.

Her mother's smile faded. "Why, it's a hope chest, Victoria. And look at the fine carving your father did along the top." The obvious disappointment spelled out on her mother's face asked Victoria to at least give her father credit for a job well done.

"What's a hope chest for?"

"For young ladies—" her father frowned "—to put in the doohickeys that they'll need as young brides. You know, tablecloths and—"

"Young bride!" Her mouth flew open; she couldn't help it. "Daddy, I'm only thirteen. Are you trying to marry me off already? I wanted a new baseball mitt. And you know that. Now you and Mom give me a hope chest?" She glanced down the flat front of her blouse. "Hopeless chest is more like it." Did her father smile or was the frown still gracing his forehead? "Wait a minute. Is this some sort of joke?" She broke into a huge grin. Of course. That was it. Her father enjoyed a good joke every now and then. Always teasing. "You got me the mitt, right, and you're just teasing me with this hopie thing?"

He shook his head, his face and ears pink with humiliation.

Playing the part of negotiator as always, her aunt pressed a smaller gift into Victoria's hands. "Maybe this will help, honey. I hope you like it." The smooth skin of Aunt Charlotte's face filled with a smile promising good things to come.

Victoria tucked a strand of her blond hair behind her ear and then opened the box. "What is it, Auntie?"

"Dear girl, why, it's a music box. See the tiny dancer on top? Wind it up and watch the ballerina spin around."

First a hope chest. Now a music box—with a ballerina. Ugh. Even though she liked to dance, baseball was her first love and they all knew it. Did no one else care or understand what she wanted?

The curtain rose and Victoria's attention switched right away to the dancers. To Phillipe. She stared nowhere but at the stage. "Oh, look." She sighed aloud, not meaning to distract. Then fingered her lips, admonishing herself. "Sorry."

Flo leaned closer, her pearlized opera glasses still aimed at the stage. "See there?" Her lips had flattened. Her face a frown. "He seems much older than his pictures. But he certainly knows how to dance. Here, take a peek." She offered the set of glasses they were to share in order to see the dancers up close.

Victoria accepted the glasses. When she looked through them, she couldn't believe her eyes. No! He was an old man. With little effort, she looked closer, seeing the difference. Those weren't laugh lines, they were canals. Why, he appeared to be Phillipe's *father* instead of the young, handsome Phillipe Mandrin from magazine covers. Maybe even his grandfather.

Bubble burst. A huge rush of air escaped her lips. So much for the dreamy Frenchman.

A nudge from the right caught her off guard. "Are you all right?"

She didn't bother to look at the man responsible for her sore toe and soiled tilt hat. "Fine, thank you."

Victoria bobbed away from the warm shoulder to see around the head in front of her. A much older woman *without* manners, merely a huge, feathered hat that flopped each time the woman nudged her husband, which was often. And why not? Phillipe was closer to the woman's age than Flo's and Victoria's. Wriggling closer to Florence, Victoria stared at the dancers. *Gracious Mandrin.* Without meaning to, she murmured, "Nothing but an old man."

"But are you enjoying the dance?" the deep voice whispered.

"Shh. Let's not interrupt the show."

He didn't say another word the entire time, and Victoria, shamed by her behavior, avoided him altogether. A man who had probably just returned from war, and she had the audacity to correct him. After all, she'd been the one interrupting the show. Well, she'd apologize as soon as the lights came back up.

* * *

Joe had known lieutenants with less authority. No one had to tell him twice to shut up. He hoped he wouldn't be facing Helga the Hun when the lights went up. He'd seen enough of her in Europe. A smile fanned his face. To be fair, there had been plenty of beautiful fräuleins, as they were called, but that one farmer's daughter, Helga Rudman, had been enough to frighten the Yanks all the way back home. They should have signed her up to fight. Whew! He chuckled to himself remembering her outspoken, aggressive behavior.

Trying hard to make out this girl's profile through the darkness, Joe could see only shining eyes, glittering eyes, beautiful pale blue eyes. Her gaze glued itself to the stage. She tucked a light curl behind her ear, and that motion struck a chord with him. A strangely familiar chord. Like seeing *the girl next door*.

Spinning around the stage, the dancers amazed him, as well. If he'd been born in a different time, a different place, with different feet, he would have loved to be a ballroom dancer, at least for fun, but he'd become an engineer. And thank goodness, all things considered with his two size-twelve left feet.

An hour later, the lights came up in the auditorium. Applause roared through the audience. What a marvelous show to come home to. Joe's hands burned from the length of the applause, but he knew how blessed he was to have come home alive instead of in a wooden coffin, to have had this experience that so many of his friends wouldn't ever know. Jimmy and John Drake, twins. Both killed, one on either side of him. Tears welled behind his lids and he shut them... tight. Squeezed out the memory of the brothers being hastily buried in an unmarked grave so no one would desecrate their bodies.

As he turned to leave, he lifted the program from the seat, and not paying attention, rammed into the back of the girl next door. "I'm sorry. I'm afraid I've been more than a bit of a nuisance tonight."

"Not to worry." Her voice carried over her shoulder, cheerful in spite of all she'd endured at his expense. She would probably get out and away from him as quickly as possible.

And then she glanced back.

His mouth nearly unhinged. That was why she looked familiar. "I guess I'll always be saying I'm sorry to you, won't I?"

Her large eyes widened. "Well, if it isn't Joseph Huntington. Ms. Davies's Dance School. All grown up." Then her eyes narrowed. "Or is that Sergeant Huntington?"

He groaned. "And I stepped on your foot...again."

Ms. Davies's Dance and Etiquette School for Young Ladies and Gentlemen. Joey had promptly stomped all over Victoria's feet until her toes must have throbbed. How could she be expected to run the bases with broken toes? He might have been two years older, but being older hadn't made him a better dancer. And she had let him know what a klutz he was.

"Watch out with those big clompers!" she complained over the music.

"Sorry, Vickie."

"And don't call me Vickie! Only my teammates call me Vickie."

"Here, here, here, Ms. Banks." Ms. Davies, her hankie fluttering nervously, had quickly arrived from behind them like the cavalry sent to save Joey. "Young lady, you shall refer to Joseph as Master Huntington, not Joey. Is that understood? And we shall not reprimand the young man in front of his peers, now, shall we?" She shook the gray springs on her head and peered over large, round glasses that rested on the end of her nose. "Not at all." Her ample self trembled with the indignation she no doubt tried to hide for the sake of propriety. Joey hadn't seen her that upset before. He had been embarrassed enough without Ms. Davies drawing attention to them.

Victoria's face blazed at being corrected. Wasn't she being corrected in front of her peers? Joey had thought it best to say nothing about that. Ms. Davies was off his back for a while, and he didn't want her to home in on him again.

Victoria, on the other hand, had plenty to say. "Of course, Ms. Davies. Whatever you say, ma'am. I don't know what came over me." Then the pale blue eyes met Joey's gaze. "And my apologies, Master Huntington."

Joey's face grew warmer and warmer still as, behind Ms. Davies's sturdy back, Victoria shot an eagle eye at him—full of daggers. The nasty old mutt at the corner hadn't given him worse.

Then, when no one was looking, she leaned in and whispered in his ear, "Just wait until you get up to bat tomorrow. I'm going to knock your head clean off your shoulders." And she nearly did.

Then she'd turned into the most beautiful girl in her class. Soft blond hair, big eyes that told you whether or not you were in her good graces.

And then the graduation dance when he'd proven he wasn't in them. Ugh.

But now here she stood, holding her gloved hand out like the lady she'd grown into. Joe barely brushed it, not wanting her to snatch it back and embarrass both of them. She lowered her voice. "It's been what? Five or six years?"

"Well, Victoria. I'd ask you what you've been doing, but that would take longer than we have standing here." He glanced around his shoulder. "I think these lovely folks would like to exit." *And so would I.* If he didn't get away soon, their past might come into the open once again. No, sir, not on your life. The last time had ended so badly; no need for a repeat of that performance. He refused to apologize again and again…even seven years later.

"Oh, of course. I'm terribly sorry." She started forward, planting her feet solidly on the walkway. "Yes, I'm sure they would like to leave."

He reached for her elbow to steady her steps. "Are you all right?"

She continued to wobble but politely removed her arm from his grasp. "Thank you. Just a bit dizzy for a second. I guess because the floor slopes here."

Her hint of a smile lit his heart, but he choked it down. Then swallowed hard again as if he couldn't get rid of the lump. She had grown into an absolute beauty. Still, her attitude told him she remembered the animosity she'd had for him all those years ago. And there was no reason to assume the feelings had changed. Why should he care, anyway? Life had moved on…for both of them.

Once they arrived in the lobby, Flo faced them. "Who's your friend, Victoria?"

"Flo, this is Joseph Huntington. You remember him, don't you? He was two years ahead of us in school." Then Victoria peered up through long black lashes. "And furthermore—"

"Oh, yes," Flo stammered. "You two have a history." She put a hand to her mouth, and her face fanned pink. "I am so sorry I brought it up."

"Nice to meet you again, Ms. Collinger." No need to go into the stormy details. He glanced at Victoria. "Yes, we have *quite* a history. Only I'd thought that now that we're adults…"

Again her attitude surfaced. "Oh, trust me. I don't give you a thought. Stepping on my feet was the least of our problems."

"I wasn't referring to the times I stepped on your feet." Now it was his turn for his face to warm at her inference.

"Nice to see you, Mr. Huntington." Florence offered dainty, gloved fingers. Her gaze didn't falter like her words.

"Please call me Joe." He swallowed hard. *Don't say another word. Stay a gentleman.* Or…wasn't that what got him into trouble in the first place with Dru Carraway?

Joe put away any negative recollections and offered to hail a cab for the ladies. Anything to make his departure; those wide eyes and full lips were drawing him in deeper, like a bucket in the bottom of a well. And he'd been down that well, getting nothing but scrapes and bruises. No reason to open the scab and bleed again.

"Thank you, but Florence's brother is picking us up."

Victoria immediately looked toward the door leading to the street; then she murmured with cold, calculated politeness, "Well, quite the surprise meeting you, Joseph. Hope you enjoyed the show as much as we did. Sorry if we *inconvenienced* you in any way. I certainly don't ever want to put anyone out." The old anger seemed to wash over her anew as if she couldn't help herself. My, but the girl could hold a grudge. And to this day she had not heard his side of what had happened at the dance. Didn't seem to want to.

He reached for her hand as the woman with the feathered hat pressed past him. "Not an inconvenience at all. Not in the slightest. Nice to have seen you again." He examined the crystal-blue eyes again for any sign of compassion, but met nothing…only a dead-on stare. *Scram, buddy boy.* "Safe trip home, ladies."

So, little Vickie Banks lived in Lansing now. Apparently no longer a pitcher. She seemed to have changed in so many ways. And in other ways, she was the same immovable, never-wrong, independent female.

At least they wouldn't accidentally run into each other now that he was home. Lansing was enough of a distance that their paths needn't cross. With that thought in mind, he struggled to figure out why he couldn't look away as those long legs climbed into a waiting auto.

Chapter 2

Joe pulled an old used-to-be-white handkerchief from his pocket and swatted at the sweat on his forehead. Would his loan application become just another entry in one of the many dusty ledgers lining the banker's bookshelves? "Mr. Flannigan, I can't very well run a construction company out of my garage. If I don't get the loan from you, there isn't much chance of launching my business. I have enough money to develop the business but not enough for a building."

"You simply do not have a solid plan." Flannigan shoved a pile of papers from one side of his desk to the other, exposing one sad pile. Pointing, he said, "Look at all of these. Applications from returning soldiers ready to start over. I can't loan you money in these times when you aren't a proven commodity. Veteran or not, you need to prove yourself first."

"Three years in the army isn't proof enough? And

a degree in engineering? I'm willing to use my entire savings along with the loan."

"Prove yourself by working in town a year or two. Then we could talk again. How about Wysse and Sons? I hear they're looking, and that seems a proper fit with your ability. Why would Howell need another construction company?"

"Mr. Flannigan, I respectfully disagree. Wysse and Sons is fast becoming a business without a leader. Old Mr. Wysse is barely taking on any new clients, and Wallace and Stephen don't want the business. They've stayed this long in order to please their father, but Stephen has plans to leave Howell and who knows what Wallace will do? He's a fly-by-night. Always was when we were in school. And from what I've heard, he's the same now."

"Well, there you have it, then. Wait until Mr. Wysse decides to sell and—"

"He'll never sell. He keeps hoping his sons will change their minds. Mr. Flannigan, I'm not about to beg you for a loan, but I certainly wish you'd give me the chance to show my mettle."

"Working awhile for Wysse first would let me see how serious you are." He wasn't without heart; Joe thought he recognized a hint of compassion in the man's eyes, but how could he convince Flannigan to take a chance on him? Perhaps the bank had experienced hard times since the war, as well.

"I don't intend to work for them. I have my father's house…my house that I can put up as collateral. I'm not asking for an unsecured loan. This company will help our town to grow. Provide jobs for the men who've returned from the war. Wysse has only hired one man. A new janitor. And he's not building houses, only commercial buildings. Please, Mr. Flannigan, if you only understood the construction business. Men returning will be taking on families, they'll need houses to move into. Don't you agree? And I'm more than capable of turning out some of the nicest little bungalows you'll ever see. Just what a fellow returning home would be looking for."

"Not at this time, young fella," he said as he tapped the pile of applications as if to remind Joe that he wasn't the only veteran wanting a loan.

Flannigan rose to his feet, extended his hand and ended the negotiations. The hope drained from Joe, through his tingling fingers of the handshake to the wobbling of his feet as he did an about-face from Flannigan's desk. He cleared his throat and turned back. "Thank you, sir. I appreciate you taking the time to see me."

"In another year or two, Joseph. You could do worse than working for Wysse. He's a good egg."

"But, sir. The need is now. Those of us in construction are already accepting that there's a housing shortage. So many men returning, nowhere to live. The moment is ripe for construction businesses. A bunch of sweet little bungalows where the men can raise families. Solid two-bedroom, one-bath places with a one-car garage to call their own. You couldn't ask for a more sure thing. In two years another company will have taken advantage and there won't be the strong need any longer."

The banker waved his hand, dismissing Joe's comment. "Not now, Joseph. Prove yourself. Prove yourself." Flannigan turned back to his desk and lifted the phone to his ear. Joe squinted at the picture on the wall above

Flannigan's head. Flannigan and Wysse shaking hands in front of a building project?

Flannigan's gaze rose and followed Joe's. His fingers quickly spun over the numbers on the phone, ending any further discussion.

"Can anyone tell me who Isadora Duncan is?" Victoria took in the room of questioning faces before her—her oldest class of dancers—modern dancers and very good. "Well? I expected you to read the biography I gave you. Did anyone do that?" She waited with a smile. "Anyone at all?"

Minnie Carlton stepped forward, a frown planted firmly on her fourteen-year-old face. "My mother said I can't read about people like her. She took the paper, ripped it up and threw it away, Ms. Banks. I'm sorry. I would have at least given it back to you, but Mother was very emphatic that your biography of Ms. Duncan not be in our home."

Smile gone, Victoria practiced her well-intentioned speech. "I certainly don't want to overstep my bounds where your parents are concerned. That's never been my plan." She gazed around at the others. "Did anyone here learn about Isadora Duncan, considered to be the mother of modern dance?"

All gazes but one fell to the floor. She'd known it was a risk to introduce such a controversial figure, but after all, Duncan led the way to modern dance, eccentric life or not. And her job was to teach these girls all she could about dance. A few discussions on manners and trying to be understanding of others didn't hurt, either. And Victoria tried her best to sneak in a few life lessons on compassion.

Manners? She shuddered. Where had her manners been that evening in Lansing? Surely she didn't continue to hold a grudge after almost seven years. She'd been so excited to be asked by a senior to his graduation dance. Then to be abandoned while he left with another girl.

Okay, so she did still harbor ill feelings. There was more than one man in the world. And her father had taught her to be treated with respect by men, not a passing fancy. She'd been *less* than a passing fancy to Joseph Huntington.

"Ms. Banks?"

Victoria's attention snapped back to the girls. "I see. I suppose I should be glad you were allowed to return to dance class at all." She picked up the biography she had painstakingly written out by hand for each girl. "Though it won't help you to understand how she became the dancer she did, I'll leave it at this." She turned aside and thought carefully about what she would share. "Isadora's parents were both involved in the arts and raised Isadora to be a…a freethinking individual exposed to many forms of art, from music to theater to dance. Rather than moving forward with traditional dance, Isadora chose to listen to the music not with her ears, but with her heart and her soul, and therefore she danced *with* the music, becoming a part of it. She had a rather colorful and, most say, sad personal life. And that is no doubt what your mothers would prefer we not discuss in class, and so we will not discuss it. All right? Only to say that much beauty in this world in the form of the arts comes from the sadness and pain in an artist's life. And loneliness. I would ask all of you, as I do when discussing any other artists, not to judge them unless you've walked in their shoes."

"Danced in their shoes," Beatrice added.

Victoria nodded. "Danced in their shoes. God is the only one who knows what is in an individual's heart. We shouldn't assume things merely by how people sometimes live. They are often clouded with bad judgment and heartache that we can't see."

She nibbled the edge of her lip, concentrating. "All right, enough said about her life. I simply want all of you to understand her idea of feeling the music in your soul and dancing to how that makes *you* feel. It will end up being different for each one of you if you allow that to happen."

Minnie spun on her toes and laughed. "I'm ready to try." She touched the arm of Carolyn, who stood next to her. "Come on, Carolyn. Let's go show 'em what we've got." The two slipped into a crouch and inched their way across the floor until Victoria leveled a stare at them. She had to admit, those two were full of life.

"I'm only offering this to my older girls," Victoria added. "You all have shown you can excel at the basics of tap and ballet and…" She glanced at the two younger girls. "Maturity. I thought you might like a chance to dance from your heart for the big recital in December. That gives us a few months to work on it. What do you say?"

Cheers erupted from all but tall, willowy Constance Whitaker. "I don't think my mother would like that." Her blue eyes filled with tears that she quickly brushed away.

"It's just another style of dance. We'll still do our tap and ballet. You more experienced girls will dance en pointe, as well. And you know how I feel about costumes. They will always be modest and proper. There's no negotiating on that, no matter what some of you see in the dance magazines. Is that understood?"

"I understand, but Mom's not exactly keen on my dancing, anyway. Sorry. I mean, she's not all that happy about my dancing." Constance turned to grab her small bag as she headed over to exit the studio. "My parents want a valedictorian in the family, so I suppose my time's better spent studying from here on out."

Victoria followed her and touched her shoulder. Constance turned. "We'll all miss you, Constance. You are a delightful dancer. I wish you every bit of success in whatever you endeavor to do." She offered what she hoped was a serious but encouraging face. "It's all any of us ever asks of you girls. No matter what you're doing, make it your best. Constance, your parents will be proud even if you don't make valedictorian, but don't give up trying. Remember, always do your best."

Wonderful advice coming from someone who hadn't done her best to be kind.

Constance's smile returned. "I appreciate all you've taught me, Ms. Banks. I really do. It's been far more than simply dancing. But studying is the priority in my home. I think the Isadora Duncan biography was just Mother's way of saying enough dance for me. It gave her an excuse to steer me toward my books. And that's all right. I love my books as much as my ballet slippers. I meant what I said. You taught me so much about… well, about life. About kindness and compassion toward others." She fluttered her hand with a gentle and sincere wave to her friends.

Victoria swallowed over a lump, nearly choking on

her memories. While she was happy Constance had taken that away from her time here, Victoria felt like such a hypocrite.

Once Constance had exited the room, Victoria tapped her stick on the table with a tad too much enthusiasm. "All right. I think we've talked quite enough. Back to work, ladies."

She understood that Duncan had been quite a controversial figure before her death in 1927, but her style offered the girls a wonderful opportunity to discover who they were as artists. Victoria heaved a huge sigh, watching the girls warm up. The beauty of dance like that of paintings, plays and many other types of artwork had long lived in Victoria's heart. Ever since dance had replaced her love of baseball.

She licked her lips, remembering the terrible time she had given her parents with a ball and a bat. Poor Father. After all, her aunt had been a tomboy and turned out just fine. But Father never missed the opportunity to remind her that men liked frilly girls. Girlie girls. Really? Ugh. Then she remembered Joe leaving her at the graduation dance. Was that because she wasn't a frilly girl like Dru? Had her father been correct? Oh, why couldn't she bring herself to forget what happened?

Now here she was, instead of being the first professional female ballplayer, teaching dance for five- to sixteen-year-olds. How life could change in the blink of an eye, but she had been correct in her thinking. Women *had* played professional ball during the war, still did. So what if her love of baseball had waned and her love of dance increased when she grew up? At least she'd been proven correct in her thinking. And if her church ever came up with a girls' team as they'd promised, she'd be back on the diamond if only for fun. She had the distinct feeling in her heart that Jesus wouldn't mind her playing one bit. That thought brought a smile to her lips.

As the older girls finished and she waited for the next class, Victoria pulled aside the utilitarian curtains in the front and glanced out the window. A tall and very dark man stood across the street in front of the bank. A familiar stature.

Joseph Huntington? In Howell? But she thought he had relocated to Lansing. And yet there he was, closing the thick wooden door of the Howell First Savings and Loan. Maybe he'd come to visit his brother and family. Maybe he'd come to… Well, she wouldn't daydream. There was a class to teach. And no dark brown eyes were going to draw away her attention.

However, her gaze refused to be redirected. She didn't miss the way the sun shone off his wavy black hair. Like a raven's wings in flight. And he no longer had the physique of a boy. But somewhere between stepping on her feet, standing her up at graduation and stepping on her feet again, he'd grown into an incredibly handsome man.

Joe couldn't have felt any lower if he'd been a worm crawling under a shady leaf. What had led him to believe he'd be welcomed back home in Howell with open arms to start his business? Just because he'd served? He hadn't earned any special place because of that.

With his folks gone, he had just his brother, Daniel, and he had to admit he wanted to be close to the family. It was Howell or nothing. After all, he'd grown up here. There had to be another way to make his business become a reality. And he wasn't about to ask his brother for help. He'd been so swell about keeping the home fires burning in Mom and Pop's house, along with taking care of the expenses. No, he couldn't go to Daniel for a loan.

He crossed the street to his car.

Big dreams. His father had taught him, go for the big dreams if you're going to dream at all. That was why he'd scraped, working two jobs to put himself through college before the war called him overseas. He'd saved every penny he could while serving, and that certainly wasn't a lot, but he'd scrimped and expected a payoff when he got out.

Big dreams. Ha!

As he pulled his drooping chin off the cement sidewalk, he spied a face peering at him from behind a curtain that swayed in front of him. He read the sign overhead:

Howell School of Dance.

Not Ms. Davies's, but Howell School of Dance. Oh, how he hoped it wasn't connected to etiquette, as well. He stared a second before seeing the curtain flap around a halo of blond hair. Could it be? No. Not *Ms. Get Off My Feet, You Clod!* She wouldn't have a dance studio. But he had to admit, from what he'd seen in Lansing, she'd turned into a beautiful woman. Why wasn't she married? She must have had tons of suitors. Then he realized, not many men over sixteen or under forty had been left anywhere in the United States. All gone to war. For what? So many of his friends had died. Well, they'd tried to make a difference overseas. Only time would tell if fighting had been the right thing to do. He hoped future generations would agree and think kindly of them.

The curtain fell into place, but his thoughts continued as he walked toward his car. Save all his money, return home alive, move into the folks' place, start his own company. One…two…three…four. No room for number five. Not yet. Not a girl, especially not *that* girl. That would mean compromise instead of his company, and he had no intention of compromising his dreams.

Besides, there was now another number five. He had to go see old Mr. Wysse and beg him for a job to please Flannigan. Not exactly part of the returning soldier's dream.

Victoria ducked behind the curtain, allowed it to flutter across the window. Was he in Howell to stay? She hoped not. She'd had enough of Joe in high school. Still, she couldn't stop the sigh that sneaked out. With those dark good looks, there was no doubt some girl had waited faithfully for his return. Probably some girl in Lansing. That must have been why he was there. All that mattered was that the girl was not Victoria Banks. No, siree…not on your life…not even…no. No matter how inviting his smile. Besides, he was likely here to see his family and then he'd be gone again. Back to Ms. Whatever Her Name Is.

Time to face facts. At twenty-three, Victoria was almost an old maid. All the great ones had been taken. She'd be teaching dance until she was as old as Ms. Davies had been. Gray coils around her head and nothing to show for her years but tiny dancers. Horsefeathers! He wasn't the only man in the world. Even though single men were pretty scarce in Howell at the moment, she didn't have to drag up old memories as if they mattered.

Then she laughed at how silly she was being since

she didn't care one bit. Not in the least. In another instant with one more peek around the curtains, she watched his retreating footsteps. She had to admit, the military certainly had not cheated him of a fine physique. He was taller than he'd been at graduation. How was that possible? And those eyes. Like the morning coffee smiling back at her from her cup, waking her. If Joe wakened her, how would she feel? Her face burned at the brazen thoughts.

Joe Huntington was handsome to be sure, and with the build of a man who would protect her for life. She'd let him get away…or had he walked away…with another girl? She sighed with audible humiliation.

All right, Dad. She should have been filling the chest with linens, beautifully crocheted items, lovely heirlooms Mom had given her. Maybe a cookbook or two. Because she certainly didn't cook very well. Her last attempt had been a burned pot roast and bread heavy enough to use as an anchor. Her only real triumphs were pies. That came easily to her, maybe because she loved pie. Cherry, apple, buttermilk, oh, any kind of pie. The taste was almost within reach. She licked her lips. But as good as pie tasted, a man couldn't live on pie alone.

Joe opened the door to his car parked a few spaces away from her school, and at the last second, turned again toward the building. She chewed the edge of her lip wondering what he was thinking. But as soon as he saw she still watched, he turned his back, hopped in and drove off. The nerve of that man. Holding a grudge after all this time. Well, it was all his fault. Not hers.

Mom always said don't take it personally if a man wasn't interested, yet this *had* become personal. From the dance all those years ago to meeting him in Lansing, where he practically made fun of her.

The old baseball mitt she kept next to the window display mocked her. She figured some lucky girl in Lansing knew how to cook, how to look girlie-girlie in order to capture a man's heart. And was probably waiting at this instant for him to return.

She pictured the perfect trim figure. A beautiful blonde with hair in her eyes à la Veronica Lake, perfect red lips and long slim hands, not fingers better suited for a mitt. Yes, no doubt waiting for him to return right at the moment. She stomped her foot at her foolish thoughts. Wasting all this time mooning over Joe. Mooning over any guy when she had more than enough to keep her life full…dance students and her friend Flo.

Move over, Ms. Davies. I'm about to turn into the town's youngest old maid.

Chapter 3

Joe tied a double-Windsor knot at his throat and glanced in the mirror. His favorite blue tie slightly crooked against a white dress shirt. He straightened it. Not bad. Not good, but not bad. It had been a while since he'd gussied up. He'd pass. Well, passing wasn't good enough tonight. He had to look handsome for her. She'd be waiting at the door looking beautiful and he had to play his part perfectly. Like the handsome prince.

He took another glimpse in the mirror. Then fiddled with the tie one more time until he had the perfect knot. There, that was better. Appearance was everything to a pretty girl. The blue reminded him of the blue in her eyes. No…no, it did not. He gave the tie a tug and stared in the mirror. Time to go.

The corsage waited in the icebox. A pink rosebud with matching pink ribbon. All for his niece, Katherine. Did little girls like rosebuds?

Katie's recital meant everything to her, and with his brother, Daniel, out of town, he had to play second fiddle, but he didn't mind. Little strawberry blonde, blue-eyed Katie was his princess for the day. And he couldn't let her down. Daniel was counting on him.

He grabbed the flower on his way out the door. Would a six-year-old think a corsage was silly? What did he know about little girls? He was a sad substitute for her daddy. And she *was* Daddy's little girl. Bobby and Kenneth, her brothers, looked forward to the times when Dad was gone. They got into all kinds of mischief—"all boy" was how Daniel excused their behavior. Snakes, frogs, stray cats and dogs. All things the boys had brought home at one time or the other, and the poor little princess had found them in her bed and on her chair. He smiled remembering all the obnoxious things he and Dan had done as young boys. Oh, yeah. Sissy Faith Meyers and the frog in her soup…and then the trip to the woodshed. That he remembered as if it had been this morning. Oh, but he and Dan had spent some wonderful times together. And now he could pay Dan back, be the stand-in father for the evening.

Yes, tonight he had more important things on his mind than the tanning his seat got for scaring Sissy Faith.

After six months with Wysse and Sons, and no personal time used, old man Wysse had allowed him to take off early so he could attend the recital. The father was a good egg, but his sons? Ugh. Wallace Wysse Jr. didn't have an ounce of ambition. And while Stephen worked very hard, he had plans to leave Howell in a couple weeks to start his own company in Muskegon. Said he loved the water and wanted a place on Lake Michigan, which left Wallace Wysse Jr. to run the day-to-day of the company. And Wallace made no bones about the fact that he wanted out of the family business. Wanted his share of the company and bye-bye. Prodigal son all over. Poor old man Wysse.

He probably would sell one day. Maybe, if Joseph toed the line, he might be able to buy out the company in time. And then one day, if he kept saving, scrimping and doing without, he might have a family like Daniel. Blue eyes softened in his mind, didn't spark anger for a change. He choked on his thoughts. Who was he kidding? Old blue eyes had held his heart in high school, and she was only prettier now. At least, she seemed so from the few times he'd seen her since he returned to town.

He checked his watch as an excuse to get moving.

After a quick trip to gather Katie and her belongings, they arrived at the studio. Nice place. New place. He didn't remember a studio being here before he left. But, then again, he hadn't been looking to take dance lessons. His nose had been planted in a book, studying.

Joe stooped to remove Katie's purple wool coat, hat and mittens. "Let's hang this up so you can go get into your costume lickety-split. We're a *tad* late. Your teacher has your costume, right?"

"Yes, Uncle Joey. She keeps them in back so we don't forget them. Thank you for bringing me. Even if we are a *tad* late." Her eyes sparkled. "And for the pretty flower." She leaned forward to sniff the corsage on her coat and hugged against his chest, the curls atop her head tickling his chin. "Thank you so much, Uncle Joey. You're almost as good as Daddy."

He kissed her sweet forehead. "Anytime, princess. Hurry up, now. Your mom and brothers will be here soon, and you don't want them to see you out front." He smoothed a curl out of her eyes. "And always remember, nobody will ever be as good as Daddy."

She waved her fingers with a wiggle as she dashed toward the back. What a precious child. *Almost as good as Daddy.* He didn't want to be almost good enough. Would he ever have a family like his brother? He hoped so.

The longing in his gut for a loving family had crept to the forefront of his mind recently. Ever since he returned from Germany. Even to the point of pushing his business plans further down the line of things to do. But how many girls were left in Howell? Most had been waiting for their boyfriends to come home from the war, and he'd left no one special behind. And he had no one but himself to blame. He could have dated, but books had been his only true companion since graduation. Since Victoria had made him feel like an ogre when he'd only tried to be a gentleman.

A gust of cold wind swirled behind him. Wallace Wysse and a cute girl blew through the door in the back...the girl from the dance production in Lansing. Corrine or Florine. No, Florence. Victoria Banks's friend. What was she doing with Wallace Wysse? Must be she lived in Howell after all, not Lansing. And she was with Wysse?

Wysse walked by and smiled in that smarmy way that he got when he thought he was one-upping those around him. "Joseph. Good to see you, old man. How goes it?" Then he lifted his nose a bit, sniffed and looked down at Joe from his lofty position. *My, he thinks well of himself.*

"Fine." Joe nodded. "*Mr.* Wysse." He smiled at Flo even though Wysse made no effort to play the gentleman and introduce her. "Florence. Nice to see you again." He held out his hand.

Her face lit up and she shook hands, apologized for how cold hers were. Wysse noticed but ignored him like a flea on the bottom of a shoe. Instead he fiddled with the neatly clipped mustache under his nose. Florence's smile, however, was sincere. "Yes, the soldier from Lansing. Did you come to see Victoria dance or one of her students?"

"Victoria?"

"Victoria…you know. My friend." Her eyes lit in a strange way. "Then you didn't? That's interesting." She ignored Wallace tugging at her arm. "Very interesting. You're in Howell for how long?"

Joe let go of her hand. "For the last six months and planning to stay."

Wysse eyed him as if wondering how they knew each other, then stepped between. "Yes, six months working for *me*. Isn't that right, old man? Just another laborer in father's company. *My* company now." He made it clear to Florence who the better man was and how lucky she was.

With a dismissive but polite smile, Joe glanced again at Florence. "See you around, Flo." She beamed. He'd bet Wysse had her along for no other reason than that he didn't want to be seen alone.

Wysse grasped her elbow and steered her away. "Don't stay out too late, Joseph. Work comes early."

Not for you. For Wallace Wysse, work didn't come at all. Joe wished the business would go up for sale, and soon, while there was still a viable company to buy.

Surrounded by sparkling hair and glittery eyes, Victoria put the finishing touches on the tutus as her littlest girls pranced about. Such darlings. With all the ribbons and feathers and bows, folks would barely notice the dances. Suki's green ribbon teetered to the side and Victoria tied it tighter into the curls on the little redhead's hair. "There you go."

"Katie, over here. Let's get you dressed."

Her older girls had created their own wonderful modern routines. All of them modest, so hopefully none of the families would be upset by Isadora's *influence*. One of Victoria's goals was to show that dance could be beautiful without being unladylike. She wanted no part of upset parents. In spite of what some studios were teaching, her intent had never been to cross the line of tasteful, and that was the way she could continue. Happy dancers with happy parents.

As she tied the bow at Katie's neck, footsteps clacked on the red-and-black linoleum floor behind her. She turned and Florence pulled her aside. "I'd like you to meet a friend of mine. Wallace Wysse, Victoria Banks."

His face lit up in a way that Victoria didn't appreciate. She looked from Mr. Wysse to Flo and back to Wysse again as he surveyed her in her dance costume. "How do you do?"

His hand covered hers in a much too familiar manner. Wasn't he supposed to be Flo's date? "Very well, Ms. Banks. I hear you're the grand dance mistress of Howell. In fact, I think my little brother, Stephen, may have gone to school with you and Florence."

Maybe he was just being friendly after all. If he knew Flo well, then it made sense he'd want to make her happy by being kind to her best friend. "I'm not sure that's what you'd call it. Dance mistress, I mean. But I do dance and these *are* my students, Mr. Wysse." Her hand waved over the curly tops before her. Then she pulled two tickets from her pocket. "Here you go, Flo. I was sorry to hear your folks wouldn't be able to come tonight."

"Mama wasn't feeling well and Daddy didn't want to leave her alone. You know Daddy." She seemed almost pleased they couldn't come. Was Mr. Wysse a love interest or merely a friend? By Flo's expression, Victoria would guess yes, Flo was very interested, but she couldn't read the escort. His stare sent mixed signals. One second he seemed enraptured with Florence, and the next made Victoria feel as if he could see straight through her costume.

She hugged her arms across her chest.

"I'm sorry," Victoria said. "I know how much your mother enjoys the recitals. Well, there's always the spring production. My mom decided not to come, either. Dad didn't make it back from the job site in time and you know Mom, the world's greatest worrier. Until she has Daddy safely home and fed, she won't stir from the home fires."

Mr. Wysse nodded. "As well it should be with wives toward their husbands. At home waiting instead of running about working. No factory worker will be bringing me *my* slippers."

Ugh. Hadn't his kind gone away with the dinosaurs? Not that she didn't think home and family were important, she simply did not see herself sitting at home pining for a man like Mr. Wysse. His slippers, indeed. And he obviously didn't approve of a woman running her own business. Victoria certainly had an opinion of Mr. Wysse, but she kept silent for Flo's sake.

After Wysse took the tickets from Flo, they walked toward the front of the small recital hall. He turned just before they exited the dressing room, pointed his finger and winked. Her stomach clenched as if snakes had somehow slithered through.

Victoria took a deep breath; she didn't have time to worry about Wysse right now and his fresh manner. Pink, yellow and pale blue fairy princesses pirouetted across the stage to the piano music of Gwendolyn Ferris. Gwendolyn's fingers, though challenged by arthritis, stroked the piano keys like a master carpenter smoothing a plank. Victoria's youngest class danced mostly in time with the wonderful music over the petals strewn on the floor. Butterflies couldn't have fluttered better or done more justice to their movements. She had to smile at their enthusiasm. Girls might dance better as they got older, but they didn't have the same heartfelt love for it as the little ones.

When Victoria peered around the edge of the curtain to soak in the crowd of excited family members, her gaze came to rest on broad shoulders. She looked up from the shoulders to the face where striking dark eyes were taking in every detail of the recital. Black hair, like frosting on the cake, topped the image. And altogether, the looks belonged to none other than Joe Huntington. What was he doing in the audience? Even now she still hadn't figured out what he was still doing in Howell.

Good looks or not, he needed to go back to Lansing where someone probably cared.

Without thinking, she pulled her sweater closer around her dance costume, covering her shoulders. How could she dance in front of him with nothing but ballet slippers and a flimsy dance costume? All right, so it wasn't flimsy, but it would still feel strange dancing before him. Then again, she couldn't send her junior girls out without their fearless leader. She had promised.

Oh, horsefeathers! What a mess to be in. She let the curtain slide back into place and leaned against the wall. Her heart pounded from…embarrassment? Yes, that had to be it. She couldn't possibly have feelings for the handsome man in the third row. It had been months since she'd seen him cross the street. So it made sense he'd returned to Lansing and was simply visiting again. But why here? Why at her dance recital? Surely none of *her* girls were old enough for him. Were they?

A drink of water would help calm the nerves; she didn't have time. She and the older group were next. Horsefeathers! As Minnie slid into position, Victoria smiled and draped her sweater over the back of the nearest chair. "Here we go. Heads up, ladies. And…smile."

They danced en pointe to the middle of the stage. Victoria trapped a sob in her chest as Minnie stole the show. Her exquisite moves and raw talent thrilled the audience until they were on their feet in the midst of applause. Victoria waited back, allowing her pupil to soak in all the admiration from the crowd; then one by one, all of the dancers joined them onstage and took a final bow. While they basked in the limelight, Victoria eased behind the curtain and quickly changed. Almost immediately, one of her older dancers slid onto the stage with long lingering strides that brought the folks to their feet a second time.

Joe searched the stage. Unless he was mistaken, that had been Victoria spinning on her toes. He was sure of it. After what Flo said, he must be right. How beautifully she had controlled the flow of dancers through their moves. Beautiful—yes, in more ways than one. But where had she gone in such a hurry? Didn't she want to take her bows along with the students? In all honesty, he wanted the opportunity to see her again. Wanted a chance to look into those huge eyes so full of wonder. She danced with the same enthusiasm and talent she'd given the pitcher's mound. Only this time, she hadn't stuck her tongue beneath her teeth as she concentrated.

He craned his neck until the woman behind him asked him to sit still. "Sorry, I was searching for…my niece. Oh, yes. There she is in front. The little pink fairy." The sudden need to explain and make excuses overwhelmed him, causing the rapid-fire comments.

"Yes…that's nice." The look she gave him said she didn't believe him and that a man sitting in an audience shouldn't be staring at little girls. He didn't know exactly what to say next, so he turned back in his seat and shut his mouth. The nerve of the woman.

She must think he was an idiot to boot. Well, he was behaving like one, ogling a woman he had known as a teenager. What must *she* think? Had she even seen him sitting here?

"Uncle Joey!" His princess of a niece didn't wait for the applause to end after the last dancer when they all took their bows; she jumped down the steps in front and ran across the auditorium. "Did I do good?"

He nodded to the woman with a smile that came across as smug, he was sure. "My niece." Then he stared into the wide eyes full of excitement. "You were wonderful, Katie girl."

"Thank you." She giggled and kissed his cheek.

He glanced to the side where his sister-in-law, Thelma, sat with the boys. "Wasn't she, sis?"

Thelma cuddled Katie in her arms. "You were the best fairy dancer ever."

The boys pulled faces and made gagging sounds with their fingers in their throats until Joe raised a brow. A Huntington expression that put fear into the hearts of many. "Treat your sister with respect, boys." *Your father might not be here, but I am, and I'll stand for no funny business.*

They sat back in their chairs, gazes on the floor and feet jiggling. "Yessir, Uncle Joe." Joe saw Kenny tug at his tie and nearly laughed aloud, but as the stand-in parent, he had to keep a fatherly expression.

Thelma buttoned Katie into her coat and tied her hat securely over her head. "I don't think we'll stay for cake and punch, Joe. Kenny had a stomachache and I don't want to take chances. After all the excitement, I'll get them into bed early tonight."

"All right. If it's okay with the princess here."

"Sure, Uncle Joey. I don't want Kenny to feel bad."

He scooped her into welcoming arms. "You really are a princess, Katie. Inside and out."

Instantly, her gap-toothed smile reached into places of his heart that hadn't been touched before. While he'd been overseas doing his part, his brother had remained behind, but he'd made a beautiful family that Joe was able to share now. There went those feelings again. If he ever got the financing to set up a company, or if Wysse committed to selling his place, he'd make every effort to meet just the right girl. If such a girl existed. Because he wanted the whole dream. The family, beautiful children and a warm house to come home to.

No sense whining about it or even thinking about that until the issue stepped up and slapped him in the face. He smiled. If he clomped on another girl's foot, his vision might very well slap his face.

Hair tickled the back of his neck. When he glanced up from the program, soft blue eyes locked on to his. His throat dried up and he had to lick his lips in order to speak. "Ms. Banks. According to the program, you are responsible for this production."

"I can't deny it. But why are you here? I have to say, it's not often we have men come off the street to partake of our performances. Not like Phillipe Mandrin expects."

"My niece." He turned toward the door in the rear, but they had long since vacated the auditorium. "Oh. I guess she's left already. I'm filling in for her daddy, though I expect I'd have been called on to come see the show anyway. She's such a sweetie, I couldn't say no if I wanted to."

Victoria put a hand to her chest. "I should have put two and two together. Of course. There can't be that many Huntingtons in town. Katherine's a darling girl."

Joe nodded. "My brother was supposed to escort her, but he was called out of town. And she knows I can't resist her. So here I am."

"Did you have any cake or punch before they left? The ladies have prepared quite the spread. I believe there are even some snickerdoodles." In spite of their history, her face seemed to invite him. No, he must be reading into her good nature. She probably offered the same kindness to any lost-looking gentleman left behind to fend for himself.

"I thought with them gone...it wouldn't be right."

Florence and Wysse appeared behind the beautiful dance instructor. Florence gasped. "Victoria, they were wonderful. You were wonderful." She tugged at Victoria's arm. "C'mon. Let's go have cake. I'm sure the parents are all waiting for you before starting."

Victoria made a face, rolled her eyes and headed in the direction of all the noise. Joe couldn't help noticing the way Wysse's gaze raked over Victoria's well-toned body. He didn't like it one bit. No, sir. Not one tiny bit.

"Wait up, Victoria. I'll have some cake after all."

Shoving past Flo and half a dozen other ladies enjoying the refreshments, Wysse handed Victoria a cup of punch. Clearly, he saw himself as some kind of loverboy. Well, not where she was concerned. How dare he leave Flo alone? She was his date, not Victoria. She also didn't care for the way he'd ogled her older dancers.

She looked down and pressed his hand away. "I think you meant this for your lady friend." But Flo saw what happened and her eyes narrowed on…Victoria? She hadn't done a thing to encourage him. She wouldn't even if Flo wasn't his date. She'd heard things, not so good things in high school. Of course, people did change, but she doubted this character had evolved one iota.

Even though Victoria snubbed Wysse, Flo stepped away and looped her arm through Joe's. Her own version of "I'm not going to allow you to treat me this way".

"Do you think we could get some punch, Mr. Huntington?" He stared for a second, and then, obviously reading the humiliation in her eyes, he took action. Hero or show-off? Victoria didn't know yet.

"Of course. I'm a tad thirsty myself." Joe patted her hand. "If you'll excuse us."

Victoria grumbled under her breath. Now she was

left with Mr. Thinks He's So Much. "If you'll excuse me, as well. I need to see to the girls." She watched Florence and Joe walk toward the refreshments. He seemed to be playing the gentleman well. Had she misjudged him all along?

Wysse cupped her elbow. "But I thought you and I might—"

"Then I'm afraid you are incorrect in your thinking, Mr. Wysse. I believe you and Florence are together this evening." Poor Flo.

His eyes roved over her once again, causing no end of discomfort as she tried to walk away. He gripped her arm tighter. "Flo and I are only friends."

"Well, that's more than we are." She offered her best phony smile that she reserved for the worst of mankind and jerked from his grasp. "If you'll excuse me."

As she passed by the rest of the folks enjoying the lemon cake and citrus punch, she didn't miss how enthralled Flo was with Joe. Was her laughter, a tad too loud, intended for Victoria or Wysse? Unable to tell, Victoria ignored it, at least she tried, by cleaning up. Dirty paper napkins...crumpled and left for dead. Busywork to keep her from wondering about the mysterious Joseph Huntington.

"You certainly are the knight in shining armor, Mr. Huntington," Flo said. "I can't thank you enough."

He smiled. "Joe, please, and not a knight, Florence. I simply can't tolerate a lovely lady being treated poorly."

Florence beamed.

Victoria picked up a stack of punch cups, half-full but deserted.

"All right...Joe." Flo blushed to her roots and beyond, if that were possible.

Paper streamers slipped from the hooks that held them and fell to the floor. Victoria snatched the last of the decorations and packed the used materials in a box. She stepped toward the back of the building but couldn't miss the fact that Florence kept her hold on Joe. She wasn't interested in him, was she? Of course, if Victoria were choosing between Joe and Wallace, she'd pick Joe, too. But he'd shown no particular interest. She bit her lip. If only… But he'd made his intentions clear enough. He had only come tonight to fill in for his brother. To encourage Katie. Not to see Victoria for any reason, which suited her just fine. She'd had her moment with him and it had ended badly.

Victoria returned to the refreshment table, and in no time at all, Wysse dropped a smirk in Florence's direction, then sidled over to claim his prize. Victoria's blood simmered, ready to boil over. He was such a cad. Didn't Flo see that? She glanced again in their direction. Still, Flo didn't seem to notice anyone other than Joe.

Flo's nose tilted upward when Wysse pressed between them. "Ready to go, Florence?"

"I don't believe I'll be riding home with you, Mr. Wysse."

Victoria saw the quiver on Joe's lips as he choked back a smile.

"If you'll excuse me, gentlemen." Flo waved a hand in Victoria's direction. "Would you care to powder your nose, Victoria?"

And with that, they strutted toward the dressing rooms in the back of the building. It seemed that Flo had figured Wallace Wysse out, but if not, Victoria planned to enlighten her even if it meant Flo's attention might be redirected to Joe.

* * *

Joe did his best to look anywhere but at the retreating footsteps. Wysse sucked air through his teeth in a near hiss as his eyes narrowed. "You don't seem to be able to keep a lady's attention, old man."

Gazing into his cup of punch, Joe smirked at the face staring back. If that's what Wysse wanted to think, so be it. "I guess you're right. My unlucky evening at that. Not like you, a woman on each arm." He made a note of switching his gaze to Wysse's empty grasp.

Joe reached for his coat, pulled it on and nodded before Wysse could comment. He glared at him. "Thing is, I came to see my niece dance, nothing more. Good evening, old man." *Calm down. You need your job. He's not worth it. You can't afford to lose the job that might make you or break you in this town.* Maybe Wysse would ignore the sarcasm.

"You'd better watch that mouth of yours, Huntington. You work for Wysse and *Sons* at my pleasure."

And the reminder.

"I have no doubt of that. None whatsoever." With a smile and a tip of his head, Joe walked away, but his teeth were tight as a twisted rubber band. Bad habit, sawing away at his jaw, but he couldn't help it. Fortunately, he hadn't been raised to act like a jerk around women, because like with the town drunk, there was only room for one in each town.

It was warm for this time of year; bone-chilling rain instead of snow drizzled over his head, cooling him down. He put his hat on, but to no avail. He'd be soaked by the time he arrived home. Dozens of others dashed to their autos, newspapers and programs sheltering their heads, but Joe relied on speed. Too little too late.

Dodging quickly, he jerked open the door to his black 1940 Chevy. A two-door. Just what he'd wanted when he came home from the war. Paid cash for it. The rubber had been good, and he'd done a wonderful job making it look almost good as used. He chuckled remembering his father's expression. In his family, you made do with good, solid secondhand if it was available, and you put in the elbow grease to bring it back to life. And in the end, that's all it really needed.

He would be glad to get home and into dry clothes, but as the motor coughed and kicked over, a beautiful woman dashed past the window. Victoria!

He cranked the driver's window down as she stopped and looked around, a drenched umbrella in her hand doing its best not to turn inside out.

"Excuse me."

She started, looked back at him. "Yes?"

"Would you like a ride?"

"Oh, no. Thank you. One of the moms will be out soon and I'll—"

"Don't be foolish. You're getting soaked. What happened to your ride?"

"Flo called her folks and that left Mr. Wysse looking for a companion. I didn't even wait to see if Suki's mother could give me a lift. I sneaked out the back and prayed one of the moms would be ready to go. I'm embarrassed to ask, but *is* there room for one more?"

"More than happy to be of assistance. Hop... No, wait." He shut off the engine and rushed around the side, hoping the car would start again. Then he opened her door and assisted her in. "There you go. Nice and dry."

He tore around to the driver's side and jumped back in, said a little prayer before starting it... Yes! First try.

"You look surprised, Mr. Huntington."

"Joe. And yes, I am a bit. I rebuilt this baby and you never know when she might decide to stop and take a nap, right about the time I need 'er to start."

"Her?"

"Well, yes."

"So a car that contrary must be a she?"

Aha! There was the attitude he'd come to expect.

And that was not what he'd meant at all. "I just… well, seems I've put my big size twelve in my mouth. I didn't mean to sound chauvinist." Time to switch gears. And quick. "Speaking of feet, you have quite the ability with dance. You always did as I recall." He grinned at his slick maneuver. No sense continuing to dig himself under.

"I see what you're doing here." A grin started on her lips, but she tamped it down quickly enough. "Nicely done, Joe. You worked that conversation much slicker than you danced. And thank you. A far cry from our days in Ms. Davies's school." For a second she seemed to relax, not dredging up the past again. Perhaps they had managed to move beyond bad memories.

"Maybe it's a far cry for you. I'm afraid I still trip over my own feet at times." At times? Ms. Davies's school hadn't helped one bit. From the dance school to his high school graduation where he had promptly clomped on Glady Hopper's beautiful glass slippers. At least, he thought they might have been glass when the heel cracked off in front of everyone. Humiliating her *and* him when she and her gigantic gown splattered onto the floor.

Victoria turned and smiled. "I am very sorry for the way I treated you in dance school."

"Just in dance school?" He returned her smile, adding a wink for good measure.

Her lips pursed, the wistful grin gone. "Well, you aren't trying to blame me for how graduation turned out, are you?" Not as far from the bad memories as he would have liked. Her attitude revisited the conversation full force. "Really."

Joe reminded himself it was just a few minutes' ride to her house if he remembered correctly.

"Victoria, I don't want to argue. That was years ago. We were kids. The fact that you wouldn't let me explain is past, way past. Let's start over, shall we?"

Her nose tilted. "*I* wouldn't let you explain?"

"No, you wouldn't. I called a dozen times or more to apologize, but you didn't even take my calls. How can a man say he's sorry if the woman won't speak to him?"

"*Mr.* Huntington. I couldn't get hold of my folks that night. I ended up going home with a young man who I thought had a stellar reputation at our school. He was kind enough to offer me a ride when you left me stranded. It turned out he wasn't such a stellar gentleman after all."

Lightning streaked across the sky and startled them both.

Joe slowed his auto, glanced in her direction. "I didn't know, Victoria, honestly."

"Apparently not, and didn't care enough to return to drive me home."

He pulled to the side and stopped his auto where mud caused the car to slip sideways; Joe refused to let it sidetrack him. "I *did* care. I tried to tell you, but you wouldn't listen."

"But you left me."

"Yes, the Filmore brothers were teasing Dru Carraway, like always, and none of the other students did anything. I had danced with her and when I went to take her back to her seat, one of the boys started again, and he said… Well, better left alone. But he was most unkind to her. So she started crying, and since she had come alone, I offered to drive her home."

Victoria's face fell and for the first time, Joe thought he saw genuine compassion. "Joe, I didn't know. Honestly." Her lip trembled.

"But why didn't you take my calls?"

"I guess I was fuming over that octopus Randy Phelps."

"The class salutatorian? That's who you rode home with?"

She pursed her lips. "The one and only. He stopped on a dark street going to my house and thought he was suddenly Casanova with dozens of hands all grabbing at once."

What had made Victoria think Randy's reputation was stellar as she'd said? All Joe's friends knew him well enough. They had called him randy Randy. But Joe didn't smile at the memory. He'd like to pound the guy if he ever had the chance. Then a reality check. That was years ago and Randy had been a kid, as well.

"I'm sorry you had to go through that. What did you end up doing?"

"I wound up my fist, pretended I had a ball in it and slugged him in the eye. Remember how that felt?" Now the grin crept over her face; whether she wanted it to or not, he couldn't tell.

"Are you kidding?" He rubbed his face. "I can still feel it today."

Then she laughed. A loud belly laugh for a girl. "You have no idea how my mother punished me when she found out about me pitching at your head. She about blew a fuse! I never could lie to my parents, and when she asked me, I had to tell the truth. I remember being quite defiant. 'Yes, ma'am. I socked him in the eye but good.' Oh, no, Joe, I have to rethink this. Between your helping Dru and not getting even after the game, you are now quite the gentleman in my book." She gave a shake of her head. "And I never thought I'd live to say that."

Rain had started to come down hard as Joe restarted the engine, again surprised that she started the first time. "You'd be shocked what I thought at the time. There might have been a toad or two caught to go in your mitt, but then I chickened out. Another trip to the woodshed I didn't want. Or need."

"A toad? I doubt you'd have been so mean." Her smile lit up the night better than the lightning. And it was all Joe could do to keep his eyes on the road. "And I hate to be the one to tell you, but toads haven't ever bothered me. I caught plenty as a kid."

"Of course you did. What was I thinking?" Joe chuckled.

Victoria touched his arm and sent jolts of lightning stronger than the strikes outside through him. "Sorry I wasn't the foo-foo little girl everyone would have liked."

"We were kids. And we thought and behaved like kids. No harm done. And I don't think being a tomboy hurt you one bit." If a black eye gave him a chance with this beauty, then so be it. And she'd finally allowed him to explain, after all these years. A huge weight lifted from his shoulders at last.

When she grinned, her teeth sparkled white against

the dark of the night. And those eyes. Talk about stars. He let out a breath. Not at all the young girl who had made his life so miserable before. And nothing like a tomboy anymore.

"I never noticed how blonde you were when we were younger."

"You saw me mostly in a baseball cap. And even so, my hair was a lot lighter then. I hated it so much. With all the curls, it made me look like a girl. Even under my cap, the curls occasionally stuck out. And I wanted so much to be a boy."

"You wanted to be a boy?" There was no mistaking it, she was very much all girl.

Her laughter filled the car. "Of course. Who wants to sit in the house learning to cook and clean when there's fishing, hunting, climbing trees? Any- and everything outside is closer to God, don't you think? Smelling the fresh air, enjoying the great outdoors."

"Couldn't you do all those things and still be a girl?"

"In case you haven't noticed, girls aren't exactly encouraged in those fine activities. Nothing about threading a needle inspires me. Besides, only by being a boy would I have gained my father's approval to play professional baseball. And that's *all* I wanted back then. Still would if I thought I could, but I'm more practical these days. And somewhere along the line, dancing slippers pushed ahead of my baseball mitt. Funny, isn't it?"

"Professional ball. High aspirations."

"Well, Dad always taught me to aim high, but he didn't realize what direction I'd been aiming until it was too late."

"And now?"

She quirked an eyebrow. "Now I'm perfectly content to be a girl. Teaching dance. Seeing these little tykes start out with two left feet, for the most part, and learning day by day to be lovely, mature dancers is such a blessing. You have no idea. Almost as good as being a babe named Ruth."

That was the truth. And a much prettier babe than Ruth. He wouldn't say that, though. What an extraordinary woman she had turned out to be. "You're right there. I have no idea about the dancing. And I'm not sure with my *big clompers* what that means for me. Guess it's a good thing I became an engineer. Neither baseball nor dancing is a requirement."

Victoria blushed and her laugh proved contagious. "But you're a smart man. You're right, not sure you'd be much of an asset in the dance studio. I should have asked you, are you happy at Wysse and Sons? I mean, after what I've experienced with the son, what's the father like?"

"I'm not particularly happy there, but it's a paycheck. The old man's all right. Good egg, really. But working for them wasn't at the top of my list." He gripped the wheel tighter as the rain and his emotions both increased. "I should stop. I've never been one to tell tales out of school. In reality, I'd always thought I would come back and—"

Lightning crashed in front of them. Joe sucked back a breath and shifted his gaze from her lovely face to outside the window. "Say, you'd better be on the lookout for your street. I can barely see in this storm. We're getting a real humdinger, wind and all." He had to be sure she arrived home safely this time. No repeats of the night of graduation. Leaving her to go home with randy Randy. No wonder she'd been angry with him.

Victoria mirrored his expression, squinting into the darkness. "There. At the end, make a right. We're the third house on the left."

A lightning strike and the sound of a bomb exploding lit up the sky. Joe accelerated.

"We're almost there!" He slowed the car and maneuvered the right-hand turn, then slammed on the brakes as they both just stared.

Chapter 4

Gazing through torrential rain, Joe didn't know who the people—silhouetted like rounded tree stumps—were. Perhaps Victoria's parents. The woman, arms over her head slapping at the rain, bawled. The man scratched his head, growing wetter by the second without so much as a sweater to protect him. Joe shook his head. They needed to get inside before they got hurt. A huge tree branch had split from the lightning strike and collapsed over the front of the house, blocking the door. The top had speared the family's roof, creating a gaping hole that let the rain inside. Why were they standing there, doing nothing?

Lightning continued its assault, rain pounding the ground into a mud bath.

"Those people should be hurrying, fixing the roof. Your folks?" They stood solid as Lot's salty wife.

Sitting deathly still herself, no doubt in shock, Victoria finally blinked…nodded. Then she rubbed the moisture from the inside of the window as if doing so might make the scene go away. "Yes, those are my parents. Oh, no." Fear focused her gaze and she finally saw all that had happened. "And our house! That branch fell through the roof!"

"Victoria, I'm sorry." But she burst into tears, unable to move from the passenger seat. He jumped from his seat and sprinted around to the other side of his auto. He opened the door, helped her out and pulled her into his arms. "It'll be all right." He wanted to believe what he was telling her. Just holding her felt right, but they were getting drenched and her parents needed to start moving. This could only get worse if they didn't act right away.

"Look at it, Joe." Her gaze locked on to the branch, which was dangerously close to rolling off the house. "Our home."

"Let's see what we can do."

His grip tightened as she buried her head in his chest. "I can't look anymore. My poor parents."

Not wanting to let go, he finally held her at arm's length and nodded. "You take your mother in through the back door and I'll talk with your father." Water ran in small rivers over the roof and into the opening. Was there any way to stop further damage to the house? He doubted they would get any repairmen out this late. But her father might have an idea.

"All right." She stepped out of his grasp, and he gave her shoulders a squeeze. "I'll see to Mom."

As the women headed around back, Joe entered the front yard, where Victoria's father had the same dazed look of shock on his face. "Sir? What can I do to help?" He clapped the man on the back. "Sir? Your house."

Her father turned slowly, his eyes watery and tired. "What's that?"

"Your roof. We need to secure your roof, cover it, keep the water out. Keep the heat in. Let's go. Time's of the essence." They had to work fast or the entire inside of the house would be ruined. Worse yet, if that branch rolled, they could lose the garage, as well.

The man shook his head, clearing it as he snapped out of his daze. He swiped water from his eyes. "Yes, of course. If you'll follow me I have tarps in the garage. Thank you, young fella." He thrust a hand forward even as his feet picked up speed. "Arthur Banks. Don't know who you are. If you're willing, follow me to the garage. I have a chain saw, but it's a two-man operation and won't be practical for the smaller branches holding the large one in place. If we're careful, maybe we can free up the smaller branches with handsaws before that branch rolls off the side and does more damage."

They were thinking along the same lines…good.

"Joseph, sir. And I'm happy to help any way I can." Arthur nodded and kept trudging along.

Joe slogged through the water-soaked ground to the building in the back, following in Arthur's footsteps. Thick mud was already forming, making a patch job really dangerous. And how could the two of them roll that huge branch off the house without creating more damage? He eyed the garage a mere three feet from the house.

Mr. Banks struggled to keep his footing and pushed up the garage door. Joe noticed his hands shaking from the cold or too much energy. That or worrying about being trapped in the garage. Dark met them, but in a few seconds, Joe's eyes adjusted.

"Over here, son. Quickly. We don't have much time, especially if that wind keeps up."

A stack of thick canvas tarps perched right beyond the door on a wooden bench. "You have so many. What do you do with all these tarps?"

Art grinned now that the shock had worn off. Rain dripped off his nose and onto the floor in an almost comic manner. "I'm a roofer. Of all things. Guess I'll earn my keep tonight, won't I?" He gazed over the heavy folds of canvas at Joe. "At least, with your help, son. Getting the trunk off without creating more problems is probably the most important right now. Let's get a move on. Lightning seems to have moved away. I don't want either of us to get hit."

As they walked out, arms full, the branch didn't seem anywhere near as big as it had appeared originally. Maybe they could do this between the two of them after all. "Then you guide me, sir. I'll be your extra set of hands and try not to get in the way."

He couldn't help a glance over his shoulder toward the back door. Blue eyes focused on him for a brief second out the back-room window. Took his breath away. Victoria had grown into such a beautiful woman. Then she turned away, no doubt to help her mother. That feeling in his stomach filled him with what? Dread? He tamped down the strange emotions. Blue eyes or not, there was work to do, and besides, getting mixed up with some girl was not on his agenda.

Victoria locked eyes with him for a second, then she twisted from the window. He had helped her father take charge and it wasn't even his home. That *was* kind. She realized now more than ever how all the problems had begun at the dance. All because Joe had been such a gentleman. But there wasn't time to think about dreamy eyes. She and her mother dashed through the mudroom to the kitchen and into the front room, their arms loaded with pots and pans to catch the water dripping from the hole in the ceiling.

"Victoria, over here," her mother shouted. "Let's protect the furniture first."

"Right behind you, Mom." She lugged the empty laundry basket filled with pans into the front room. "Here you go."

They set a pan under each drip.

At last, her mother took the time to stop. "Who's the young man?"

"Joe Huntington." Victoria bit down on her lip.

"Who?" Her mother's voice changed almost immediately, her lips pursing, exposing her agitation. "Isn't he the boy who—"

"Not now, Mom. I'll explain later. But it wasn't at all what I had thought." She shook her head. "Not at all. So put away that angry face and let's get this done."

Victoria set the biggest pot on the sofa cushion to keep off the water. Then realized that moving the sofa worked better. So she slid her arms around the top and heaved it out of the way.

Her mother's brow was still knitted together, a face Victoria had been on the receiving end of too many times. Oh, yes. She was remembering Joe, all right. Was she also remembering how she'd been in trouble at dance school with Joe? Her mother had been required to talk with Ms. Davies about Victoria's behavior. *Horsefeathers. Not another lecture now, please.* That was years ago. She was a grown-up now.

But Joe pushed through the front door before her mother could respond. "Here you go. Mr. Banks said to cover the furniture. I'll help." He took control immediately and Victoria liked that. A decisive man. "We're going to be cutting the limb, and you'll both need to get out of the house, just in case."

Her mother eyed him suspiciously but managed to ask, "In case of what? Is there another disaster ahead of us?"

"No, ma'am. But we don't want to take chances when we roll that branch off the roof."

"Oh, my." Her mother's hand fluttered over her chest. "Off the roof? Where will you roll it?"

"Ma'am, there's room on the other side of the house between your place and the neighbor's. He's out helping us, too. We've got ropes rigged so it shouldn't fall on the garage."

"On the garage?" Her mother's hands started their telltale wringing, a sign she was about to fly over the top.

Joe seemed to recognize her anxiety and moved her toward a dry chair. "Sit for a minute. Let me help Victoria. We'll cover the sofa right away. Victoria, move those pans near it and we'll put on the cover before it's completely ruined." He opened the tarp up and spread it out. "Why not push the big pieces together? This is big enough to cover all of them."

He didn't wait for a response but shoved one of the chairs toward the sofa.

"I can't sit here and do nothing." Her mother rose and took an end of the tarp. Maybe his helping would let her see him in a different light. "Don't worry, young man, I might behave like a fainting flower from time to time, but I'm stronger than you think." She slapped her hands. "What should we do first?"

Joe and her mother tucked and pushed until they had the tarp secured over most of the front room furniture. The rest of the smaller pieces didn't seem to be getting wet, so they just corralled them tighter to the far wall and set out more pans.

With his jaw tight, he started for the door. "There you go. I'm headed back up on the roof with your father."

"On the roof?" Victoria shouted. "You shouldn't be up there in your dress clothes. Those shoes will slip and slide. Look at all the mud on them. You could get hurt!" She followed him to the door, where she bent down, grabbed a glove from the umbrella rack and scraped at the mud. When she stood back up, her face zinged with warmth.

"Aw." He clipped her chin. "You care about me." He dropped a smile, then dashed out the door. "Your father needs my help, dress shoes or not. I can't leave him up there by himself. *That* would be dangerous."

"But, Joe…"

He grinned like a cat with a mouse, but his face quickly reflected his concern for them. "You ladies should get coats on and sit in my car. It's out of the way. Your neighbor is helping us prune the smaller branches, but we don't want her to roll until it's time."

"Her again, huh?" And with that she headed for the coatrack.

"Yes, ma'am. Definitely a *her*. How about if you two get under cover before we start the heavy work? Don't want any mishaps."

Victoria drew in her lip with her top teeth and bit down…again. How chivalrous. Was he as wonderful as he appeared to be, or was this the face he donned for her parents? Who was the real Joseph Huntington? One minute cold as ice, the next giving her a ride home, apologizing, helping her father. She shook her head. Too much mystery for her to care. So why the fluttering insects in her stomach?

Joe stifled a chuckle. His shoes? Was she really concerned with his shoes when she had a five-foot section of her roof ripped away? He'd been through war and back, and he understood that clothes could always be replaced, but a man's life came along only once. Determined steps drove him out of the front room toward the back and around to the outside front of the house again, where Mr. Banks and his neighbor were mulling over the fall of the branch.

As he lifted his feet in the mud, they dragged like lead weights. The mud crusted the edges so that they looked more like shoe boxes than shoes. He shook off as much as he could, then scraped them against a broken branch.

"Son, grab that big tarp off the hood of your car." Art nodded. "That's the one. Lug it up here. Be careful, now. Those shoes are gonna be slippery."

Okay, so maybe she was right about the shoes. He'd be a bit more careful.

An hour passed as Joe, Mr. Banks and the neighbor named Slater cut the huge branch away from the house. Then with Mr. Banks on top and ropes fashioned to help it fall in the right direction away from the garage, Joe and Mr. Slater eased the branch over the side and onto the ground with a bang. Then the three of them created a sort of canvas roof by tacking all the edges so the wind and rain couldn't penetrate the ceiling anymore. That should protect the home until the storm subsided.

Art offered a muddy hand by way of thanks. "Bob, thanks for your help. Without you and Joe here, I don't know what I'd have done." Slater reminded him that he'd be by in the morning and help him cut up the branches into firewood. Art turned to Joe. "Young fella, I think you'd better come in and warm up before heading out."

Slater waved and left for home.

"Thank you, sir, but I should probably skedaddle." He didn't need another look at blue eyes. Did she believe what he'd told her? He hoped so. Then maybe she would consider…no. No, he was married to his plan, not to the idea of dating. Not yet.

Art clapped him on the back. "We wouldn't hear of it. Some hot coffee and a piece of my wife's pumpkin pie, if it isn't soaked through with rain. Guess I shouldn't offer till I know for sure, should I?"

Being neighborly would go a long way in establishing himself back into the community. And pie sounded mighty good. "Well, if you insist. Sounds good even if it is soaked."

Joe's eyes lit up as he followed his nose to the back of the house, where it was dry and smelled of coffee and spice. All gentleman, inside and out, Banks had made it clear that Joe shouldn't leave without a proper thank-you. Now he was glad.

"Here's a boot scrape for your shoes. Although I can't imagine Mother being upset about a little mud at this point." His laughter belied the fact that his house still suffered from the storm.

Victoria rushed into the kitchen and waved a hand toward them as they scuffled in. "Mom and Dad, I suppose official introductions are better late than never. This is Joseph Huntington. He came to my rescue this evening to bring me home after the recital."

"Don't I remember you hanging around the house when you two were younger?"

Joe swallowed hard. "Yessir. I took Victoria to the graduation dance."

"That's it. I remember. Well, well. Now, isn't that interesting?" Mr. Banks looked from Joe to Victoria and back again. "Very interesting."

"Am I still welcome to have coffee?" He chuckled, hopefully breaking any tension that cropped up.

Her father slapped Joe's hand into a tight grip. "More than welcome. And your timing couldn't have been any better, could it? You rescued more than my daughter. I'm much obliged, son."

Her mother's frown as she cut the pie distressed Joe. Was she remembering how he'd left their daughter at the dance? Then she stopped the frown and put on a smile, for his sake or for her daughter's?

"Oh, Victoria, was it a good show? I'm so sorry we had to miss it. When Daddy didn't get home in time, I was so worried. I couldn't very well leave until I knew he was all right and had some supper. And now I'm thanking the good Lord that we didn't go. This might have been much worse."

"It was lovely, Mom. Besides, you and Daddy saw the dress rehearsal last night. I think it might have been even better than the show. How many times can a person watch fairy princesses dancing about the stage?"

"Well," Mr. Banks chided, "you know better than to

think we'd miss a single one of your spiffy dance productions unless we couldn't help it."

Victoria pecked his check and handed him a piece of pie. "I do know. You and Mom are my biggest fans." She turned to Joe. "Well, I didn't ask you. What did you think of my *spiffy* dance production?"

"I think my niece is a prodigy." He grinned. "And her teacher is wonderfully talented." Those eyes again, narrowed right on to his gaze. He looked away. Because he'd love to say more. Tell her how beautiful the teacher was.

She laughed. "That may very well be." Her blush sent his heart to beating loudly enough that her parents must have been able to hear it. "I mean, about your niece. Time will tell if she continues to practice and move up. But she was adorable, wasn't she? And always very determined to learn each and every step until it's perfect. That's a lot for one so young."

Her father mumbled something about it being better than playing baseball, but Joe knew enough not to take the bait. Still, his eye twitched.

Instead he took a seat and slid his fork into the flaky crust and then the creamy pumpkin. "This is delicious pie, Mrs. Banks. Thank you. Just the right amount of cinnamon. My mom used to put in too much, but this is about perfect." He frowned at the memory and recovered in time to offer a second smile of approval.

Victoria's mother put a hand to her heart. "Used to?"

"Yes, ma'am." He swallowed hard. "Both my folks are gone."

A stillness settled over the gathering. Even the storm outside had finally moved along. "That's right. I remember reading about the accident. I'm so sorry, Joseph."

The four finished their coffee and had seconds on

the pie. They had discussed the recital again and Joe's precocious niece. Contentment overwhelmed him as he began to see a different side of Victoria. Not the little diva he had always imagined her to be. And her parents, well, they were the salt of the earth, as his mother would have said. Good folks…kind folks.

Joe accepted the warmth the family offered. He hadn't felt this at ease in years except at his brother's home where he was treated like royalty. "I do appreciate your hospitality."

Victoria's mother spoke up. "And well you should be on the receiving end after all the hard work you did with my mister. He'd have had a difficult time covering that roof by himself. And even more trouble with the branch. You and Bob Slater saved the day."

Art said, "Two women certainly wouldn't have been much help."

Victoria rolled her eyes.

Was she still as tough as she'd seemed as a kid? Or had she merely filled the role of son so many times the habit was hard to break. Joe remembered her being an only child.

"We're all grateful." Mrs. Banks dropped a hushing glance at her daughter.

"Anyone would have done the same, ma'am." Not Wallace Wysse Jr. Not unless there had been something in it for him, of that Joe was sure.

Chapter 5

Joe leaned over the latest blueprint for the new office building on Main. He'd worked on this project for two weeks now. Ever since the night he'd helped the Banks family. He could do this job cheaper, better and more reliably than Wallace Wysse Jr. Whatever had made that man think he could be directly involved with the building? Joe understood how to coax good work out of folks: work right alongside. Wallace only knew how to boss.

Someday, when Joe had his own company, things would be different. As he sharpened his pencil to take notes, he noticed old man Wysse standing near the loading dock in back, hands tight at his sides. What the…?

Joe casually strolled to the window in time to see Wallace shaking his finger in the old fellow's face. Joe cracked open the window.

"I won't have you selling the business out from under me, Father."

"But you said you didn't want the headache. And Stephen couldn't care less."

Wallace took a step back as if evaluating the situation. "That was before."

"Before what, son? What has happened to change your mind?"

"Joseph Huntington happened, that's what. Why you hired him in the first place is beyond me. The guy's useless."

"Useless? As in, knows what he's doing. Son, really."

Joe was a problem between Wallace and his father? Whatever for? He worked harder than any of the other men here. Wallace should be grateful, not angry with him. Perhaps he was only interested in getting his own way. If Joe remembered correctly, Wallace had been like that in school.

Wallace pressed forward. "He wants to start his own business, but I heard the bank won't loan him any money. That tells me plenty. You trust Mr. Flannigan, don't you? See? So, I'm guessing with all that failure attached to him, he wants *my* business."

Mr. Wysse cocked his head. "You mean my business, don't you?"

"You know good and well what I mean, Father. Besides, I'm thinking it's a good idea for me to take the company over after all. Keep it in the family. I know that's what you've always wanted."

With a shake of his head, the old man ambled back toward the door to the dock. "I never would have believed it, son. No. Not on your life. You were raised better than this."

Joe closed the window and scuffed the floor with his shoe. Did Joe really dislike Wallace because Wallace wasn't a good worker? Or were there other issues at hand? The fact that Wallace had singled out Victoria to try to impress.

Like it or not, he needed to have a talk with the senior Mr. Wysse.

After a day of wrangling with his emotions, Joe found himself outside the old fellow's door. His belly churned. As much as he hated confrontation, he had to try. He just had to.

The welcome greeting following his light rap put his mind somewhat at ease. Joe entered and shook Wysse's hand. He seated himself opposite the huge desk in the company office. "I'm sure you know why I'm here, sir."

"For a raise, I suppose. Is that it, young fella? And no one deserves it more than you. Joseph, you've been an asset to us." The old man's eyes looked tired. Pouchy and red.

The chair grew colder under Joe's rump; he fought to get comfortable. "Well, sir. I had actually wanted to talk with you about a more serious matter than a raise."

"What's that? What could be more serious to a young man than a raise?"

"Buying you out, sir."

"Buying me out? What gives you the idea I want to sell my business?"

"Honestly, sir? Since I moved back home I've heard rumors that Stephen has no desire to stay in Howell, and Wallace has made it abundantly clear that he wants out of the business. And I can tell by his lack of attention at the job that—"

"Hold up there. Best to say no more on that topic.

Wallace is my son. He and I have discussed the matter, and it seems he's ready to step up and take the reins from me. I've looked forward to this day for a very long time." But his face said differently. He was just putting up a good show for Joe to keep his son's reputation intact.

Interesting. Yet no need to let on to the old man that he'd heard the conversation. "I had no idea he was interested in running your business. I apologize if I spoke out of line." Out of line and now probably out of a job. At the least, he'd put an end to any hope of ever having a chance to one day purchase the company.

Wysse offered a strained smile. "No harm done. But I'm sure you can understand that I have always wanted my business to pass to my sons, now my son. So we'll forget we had this conversation, and I'll wish you the best. See you back on the job?"

"Yessir, you will." *Until I can figure out a way to convince the bank to loan me the money I need.* He would certainly like to do business with the old fellow, but if it came down to Wallace one day selling, Joe wouldn't trust the ink the signature was signed with. No, if he couldn't have a sale while the senior Mr. Wysse ran the show, he didn't want it at all.

Joe felt like a dog skulking away with its tail tucked. He had to find the means to start his own company. And with the way he felt when he was around Victoria lately, he also needed to keep a sound distance between them. A woman meant nothing but trouble for his plans. Even one as out of this world as Victoria Banks.

He caught his lip between his teeth, mulling the truth. And the truth was he'd love nothing more than to let her be part of his plans if he had the financial means to take care of a wife. He couldn't ask her to merely be a part of grand schemes that might never take place.

Victoria sprinted up the stairs, her hair flying in her face. At the top she stopped, caught her breath and sprinted to her room. She sat on the bed, longing to let go of her good upbringing and scream. She had agreed to a meeting with Wallace Wysse Jr. Ick. Why had she? Who was she fooling? He had mentioned that he had a question he wanted to ask Flo but needed to speak with Victoria first. Was he really going to propose? He didn't act as if he even cared for Flo. And Victoria didn't like him one smidge. Too pushy, too fresh. Still, he might want her advice. He had said as much. He might be planning to buy Flo a ring.

Oh, horsefeathers! She wasn't going out with Joe; why not have dinner with Wallace? She slumped onto her bed. What had made her say yes? Maybe because Joe had been so cool lately. She'd thought after their talk the night of the storm that things would be different. That he might see her differently. Although he had been very up-front about the fact that his future company meant more to him than anything else. So she didn't owe him any explanations about meeting Wallace. Where had that thought even come from? She didn't owe him so much as a howdy. But still she felt guilty, as if she were somehow sneaking around.

Flo would be furious if she found out and thought this was a date, at least until she knew why Victoria had accepted the invitation. She only wanted Flo to be happy, and if this helped move things along, then so be it.

Victoria still didn't understand what Flo saw in Wallace. Then again, Flo hadn't ever been sensible when it came to men. She didn't think enough of herself to be choosy. Well, Victoria was choosy. And she certainly wouldn't let a man treat her the way Wallace treated Flo. But to each his own.

"Victoria? You upstairs getting ready, sweetie?"

"Yes, Mom. In my room. But I'm not busy. You need something?"

"Could you please come get your basket of clean clothes and put them away? They won't jump in the drawers by themselves."

"Yes, ma'am. In a minute." Last thing she wanted to do was her laundry—a nap was all she really wanted. She'd been so tired lately, what with the recital and all. But chores had to be done. After all, she lived with her parents and that meant no free rides. How she desired her own place. She groaned. The dance studio had a ways to go before she considered herself in the black. Maybe next year once she opened the class up to even older students. Students whose mothers wouldn't be hovering around analyzing her dance philosophy.

She jumped up quickly, too quickly, before stumbling down the stairs. Lugging the basket up, one step at a time, she had to stop halfway to catch her breath. She must be coming down with something. Never in her life had she been so thoroughly exhausted. She could beg off meeting Wallace. A phone call would do it. No, she had to be fair. No more misunderstandings like with Joe. Always think the best of people, right?

She took her time folding and arranging her clothes in the dresser. In no hurry to primp for the evening, she rested on the edge of the bed where eyes as dark as thick molasses filled her head. They smiled, they focused on her, they switched to standoffish in an instant. One second crinkling in the corners and warming her through and through, the next second, targeting a place far past her. A place where she wasn't welcome.

She slumped against her pillows until she managed to banish Old Molasses Eyes from her mind. Mostly. If only he would let her know how he really felt. She'd spoken with him just once since the night of the recital. He had run into her at the five-and-dime as she waited for Flo to be finished with work. One small salute and a cursory greeting, and he'd strolled past with the hint of a smile, nothing more. Another time he'd waved from across the street, then walked briskly on. How had the boys said it when they were little? Girls had cooties? That's how she felt around Joe, on and off as if she had cooties sometimes.

With a laugh, she moved to the vanity her father had built when she turned sixteen—no doubt another attempt to girlie-girl the ballplayer out of her—and sat on the padded chair. She ran a brush through her hair again and again, forcing the last tangle to flee. When in actuality she cared not one whit whether or not her hair had tangles in it. Did she want to look good for her meeting with Wallace? Not particularly. He'd asked the favor at a weak moment. Stinking weak moments. Maybe she'd simply pull her hair back and tie it with a ribbon.

"Better get a move on, Dolly," her father shouted from downstairs. "Your gentleman friend will be here any minute."

He's not my gentleman friend. He's not my anything.

She eyed the baseball prominently displayed on her dresser. If only... But why waste time whining about what might have been? She loved dancing, almost as much, yet when she thought of the women who played during the war, her mind instantly returned to the bases. The wind blowing over her cap as she stood on the mound, the windup, the pitch. *Crack!* A broken bat because the fabulous pitcher pitched a fastball. Nice dreaming.

Still, she might have been a Rockford Peach, or a Racine Belle. No, her parents would not have allowed that. Recently, she had heard rumors that Kalamazoo was considering a women's team. At the very least, she'd go watch them once. A Michigan team. What a lark. She breathed in the sweetness of all her memories.

"Victoria, someone's at the door."

She huffed, "Coming." Victoria threw a sweater over her blouse and slid her wool coat from the closet. Gloves? Where had she put them? Downstairs by the front door.

Her feet danced down the stairs, but before arriving at the bottom, she remembered herself and behaved. "Mr. Wysse. Nice to see you again." Not really. But anything for a friend.

"I won't be late, Dad." She stepped into the cold with Wallace's hand on her elbow to keep her from slipping on the icy walkway.

"Where are we going, Mr. Wysse?"

He smiled, and she had to admit he wasn't bad looking when he wasn't frowning.

He reached for her hand, but it made her feel uncomfortable. He ignored her hesitation as he laid on the charm and said, "Call me Wallace, please. I thought, perhaps, the Dusty Rose downtown. They have luscious steaks and homemade ice cream for dessert. Even in the winter, I can enjoy a bowl of their butter pecan."

"We could just have coffee at the diner."

"Nonsense, you're doing me a favor. The least I can do is treat you to a decent dinner." Did he think her mother shortchanged her?

He helped her into the car, but she breathed a sigh once he let go of her arm. There was something about him she simply did not cotton to. He said and did all the right things, but when push came to shove, her skin crawled around him. Like a snake. Thankfully, this would be the first and last meeting with him. If he didn't get whatever answers he wanted, too bad.

Rather than start his car right away, he leaned back against the seat and stared at her. "You do realize this is one of the few 1942 Ford Super Deluxe coupes that was made before they stopped production, right?"

She squirmed until she couldn't stand his gaze any longer. "I'm afraid I wouldn't know one auto from another, Wallace. Well, we'd better go. I have to be in by nine."

Deflated like a burst balloon, he whined. "Nine?"

"The price one pays for living with one's parents. I also have classes tomorrow. Besides, I wouldn't want Florence to get the wrong idea."

"I had thought we might take a ride after dinner. To talk. About Florence, that is."

The look in his eyes unsettled her. There wouldn't be any ride, and she was quite happy that she still lived at home where folks expected her at a certain time.

Joe tugged the tie away from his throat until the knot relaxed. Then he sliced another piece of the juicy beef. Dusty Rose had the best roast beef dinner in town. And reasonable. Not that he didn't cook, and cook well, but every now and then he liked to have a home-cooked meal, and the cooking here lived up to Mom's apple pie. Speaking of which, he'd finish his meal tonight with pie and a scoop of vanilla ice cream. His mouth watered. His mom sure had made great pie.

Oh, how he missed the folks.

Moments like this offered a glimpse into the past. His parents, his brother, a life with a happy family. Then the accident and all of that ended. One minute his parents had left their club meeting, the next a truck had run them off the road. He could still recall the raw pain of losing them.

He swallowed over the clump of food in his throat. Nothing stayed the same forever. Happy came and went like anything else. A solid business was the only sure thing a man could count on, and Joe planned to have his own company sooner rather than later. That meant sticking to his decision to have the business established before the girl. But if he waited too long, he could lose her.

There it was again. Why couldn't he dash her from his mind? The two times they'd seen each other since the storm, he'd done his best to put aside any ideas she might have about him. And it did him good as well to remember what his goals were. Dating would be unfair. He had little to offer other than a house that needed a lot of elbow grease.

Well, no sense dwelling on that now. He attacked his plate again. The honey-glazed carrots melted on his tongue. And the dark brown gravy over the potatoes, sheer delight. With a wife, he'd have home-cooked food every night. The ability to make a delicious pie would be a must.

He'd also have mountains of responsibility. Certainly a child or two. And without enough money, he'd struggle to take care of them. No, he didn't need complications. Just a plan. He'd count his pennies until he started the company. And then he'd count them even more.

Joe finished his dinner and looked up as car lights shone through the window. Other hungry pilgrims out in the cold arriving to warm their insides. They'd find plenty to eat here.

A couple of minutes later, the door blew open along with a blast of icy air and a small dusting of snow. A man and woman entered. The woman turned...glanced over. Victoria. And Wallace Wysse.

"Check, please!"

Victoria's cheeks warmed when she glimpsed Joe sitting at a table toward the back. His gaze locked on to hers for the briefest of seconds. Of all the places Wallace had decided to come for their meeting. Had he planned this? No, no one would be that unkind.

"Joe, old man. How goes it?" Wallace shouted all the way to the back.

Joe's face zinged red at the mention of his name, but he nodded, then returned to his food, frowning into the plate. The waitress passed by, dropping a tab by his hand after which he immediately stood, laid money on the table and headed for the door. He had to pass right by them, and Victoria shivered at his closeness.

"Wysse, Victoria. Roast beef is especially good tonight. Have a nice evening."

Right to the point, no sentimental platitudes. Mortified, Victoria moved aside. Her feet nearly galloped after the waitress, who guided them to a table away from the door.

"Will this do?"

"Perfect," Victoria said.

Wallace, of course, had to be contrary. "I had thought closer to the door."

But Victoria wasn't known for shyness. "If you don't mind. It's a little warmer over here." She tugged her sweater closer around her shoulders to prove the point.

"Of course. I hadn't thought of that." He patted the sweater on her arm, his touch causing her to pull away, and he couldn't help noticing. "Did seeing Mr. Huntington upset you? I'm sorry if it did. We could always go elsewhere. Nothing carved in granite says we have to stay here."

"Not at all. He and I have known each other since we were children. We're friends."

"I thought perhaps—"

"Just friends." She walked toward the seats and sat down.

His gaze narrowed as if trying to discern more, but at last, he let it go. The plump waitress with a tag that said Carmen had joined them and waited while they perused the menu. "Then why don't we order? I was thinking a nice, juicy steak."

Carmen smiled. "That's delicious, but our country chicken with dumplings is the specialty today, and very good. Falls right off the bones. And the dumplings are, pardon the cliché, light as feathers."

Victoria smiled. "Ooh, that sounds wonderful. I'll have your chicken with dumplings, please. And a glass of milk." She put her hand out. "And maybe applesauce? That sounds good."

"Milk!" Wallace's eyes widened. "Not too daring, eh?"

Carmen, glasses teetering on the end of her nose,

tapped her pencil on the pad. "The chicken is wonderful, miss. I'm sure you'll enjoy—"

"Thank you." Wallace waved her away. The woman might have been a fly brushed off a piecrust. "If you'll give us a minute."

She raised an eyebrow, gazed at Victoria with a look that asked her permission to leave. Victoria nodded and smiled. "Thank you for the suggestion."

Wallace placed his fingers over her hand and she pulled away. "I planned to treat you to the best. I thought—"

"And I thought you would want me to order what I like." She wrung the napkin in her hands for a second, feeling her eyebrows knit together, but she could give as good as she got, and tonight would be no different. They weren't here to argue over food, just for a meeting about Flo.

"I can see I should have ordered for both of us."

"I beg your pardon?"

"Women can be so indecisive with what they actually want." His gaze drifted across the room, landing on the seat Joe had occupied just seconds before.

Victoria licked her lips as all the muscles in her face tightened. "Wallace, this isn't working. I found you terribly rude to that woman. She was just trying to be nice. Simply doing her job. And now you're being incredibly patronizing to me."

"She was butting in."

"No, she was offering a suggestion. And one I was grateful for."

He jerked his hand to his lap. "I'm sorry. I wanted to make this a night on the town for you. But it seems seeing that Huntington fellow has spoiled it all."

"We aren't out for a night on the town. You said you needed to ask me about something where Florence is concerned. Now you act as if we're on a date. That couldn't be further from the truth. And Joe had nothing to do with this. The problem seems to be your attitude. You are rude to people. You were rude to Flo at the recital, and you were unkind toward Joe. I honestly am not sure why I agreed to this meeting knowing that, but I did. I apologize. It seems the two of us have very little in common. And for the life of me, I don't see why you need to talk to me about Flo. You and she should discuss your own problems."

His face had turned almost purple and Victoria thought it best to stop talking. The waitress had continued to step farther and farther away and was now practically in the kitchen. Victoria had made a scene. "I'm sorry, I didn't mean to embarrass you, but this was a foolhardy idea," she said in a low voice.

"I'm not used to being treated like this, Victoria. I would think you'd be pleased to have the son of Wysse and Sons take you to dinner. After all…" He raised his eyebrows and struck a pose in the chair across from her.

"After all what?"

"Well, you aren't exactly a teenager. How many other men are knocking at your door?" He continued to smirk.

He did not just say that, did he? She jumped to her feet. "You are incredible." Did he think he was a prize catch or something? Well, not on her line, he wasn't. She'd throw him back in. Too small. At least in integrity. "I was very clear this is not a date. And I'm so grateful for that fact. You would be the last person in the world who—"

The door opened and Joe stepped back in. He checked the coatrack by the door and then walked toward the back. "Hey, Carmen. Did I leave my hat here?"

The waitress stepped around the counter, hat in hand, as Victoria rumpled her napkin and plopped it on the table. Carmen lifted the hat and said, "Here you go, Mr. Huntington. I thought I should put it away, just in case."

"Carmen, I've told you to call me Joe. You make me feel like an old man calling me mister."

"All right, Mr. Hunting—Joe." She smiled. "Try and remember your hat next time. I feel like your mother picking up after you."

Wallace winced at Joe's familiarity with the waitress and raised his voice to Victoria. "He fits right in, doesn't he?" He made a disagreeable face. "With the help and all."

"I think I'd like to go home, Mr. Wysse." Her hands rested on either side of her hips.

"Well, I came to eat. You might as well order. Chicken, if that's all you want. And *milk,* remember? And if you aren't going to eat, then just sit until I'm finished."

Victoria huffed as Joe and the waitress moved past her. Victoria laid a hand on the woman's arm. "Miss, I'm sorry to be a bother, but would you mind terribly if I used your phone?"

"Why, of course not. It's no problem at all. Is everything all right?"

Joe held out his hand. "May I be of any help?"

That would be wonderful, but no way would she put him out because she'd been a fool. "Thank you, but I think I'd better call my folks. I need a ride home and—"

"I'd be happy to see you home." His gaze slid over her head and landed on Wallace. "Victoria? Did he do anything? Say anything inappropriate?"

"No. I'm fine now, if you really don't mind, taking me home, that is."

"I'd be happy to." He glanced again at Wallace, who stayed seated throughout the entire exchange only glancing from the corner of his eye. "But aren't you with—"

"Not any longer." *Not ever again.* "I'm sorry to impose like this. But I'm afraid I'm not feeling well."

Carmen patted her hand. "Take him up on it, sweetie." She leaned closer so only Victoria could hear. "He's the better of the two. I know them both. You go on with Mr....Joe here. And I hope you feel better."

"I'll do that." Victoria reached for her coat, wondering how desperate she must seem to Joe. Did he think she'd planned to do this once she'd seen him? Well, she would clear that up right away. No more misunderstandings, not tonight.

Wallace tipped an imaginary hat. She realized he had intended for this to be a date after all.

Not on your life.

Joe tensed at her side, but she put a hand on his arm. "Could we go—now?" She grasped his arm tighter, holding on to keep herself upright. The room swirled for a second, then stopped. "I'm afraid I haven't eaten since breakfast. I'm a little dizzy."

The waitress offered to fix her something right away, but Joe intervened. "Let's get you home. Your mom will no doubt have supper waiting if she's anything like mine was. And if not, we'll raid your icebox." He grinned, showing beautiful, straight white teeth. She hadn't noticed before what a truly magnificent smile he had.

Flutters rippled through her stomach.

Chapter 6

Victoria settled against the high-back chair in the kitchen and bit into her chicken salad sandwich. "Mmm. Grapes and pecans, my favorite, Mom. Thanks. I was hungrier than I thought."

Joe smiled at her hearty appetite.

"Joseph, dear, how about you?" Her mother had a plate headed his direction.

"Thank you for offering, Mrs. Banks, but a piece of cake will be plenty. I was finishing dinner as Victoria arrived at the Dusty Rose. However, I didn't get my dessert and that cake smells wonderful. Can't resist." *I can't resist your daughter, either. Did I say that out loud?* He glanced across the table at long blond hair pulled back with combs at the top of her head. Her hair had been lighter when they were younger; now it was a smidge darker with a hint of red in it. But those pale blue eyes sparkled at him over the top of her sandwich.

Had there ever been a more beautiful girl? He sighed. She deserved better than a man who knew very little about women, just enough to stomp all over their feet.

She deserved, at the very least, a man who made a decent living and could take care of her.

He forced the feelings deeper into his gut where he could control them. No woman. Not now. Huntington Construction Company was the only thing that mattered. Eat the chocolate cake, accept the gratitude for the ride home and scoot out the door. With a tug at his collar, he accepted how difficult that was going to be.

Eyes bright and full of warmth, Mrs. Banks grinned at him. "Dear boy, you were her knight in shining armor. You have all the cake you want. Whoever heard of a man asking a girl out and treating her like that?"

Her words stuck in his throat. Victoria might have forgiven him, but had he forgiven himself?

Without realizing what she'd said, Mrs. Banks cut into the chocolate fudge cake and plopped a generous piece on the plate in front of Joe. "Coffee to go with it? Or milk?"

"Coffee. You're very kind."

Victoria seemed to read his mind. "Joe, you are the one who's kind. Talk about coming to the damsel's rescue. I'm not sure what I'd have done if I had to spend one more second in Wallace Wysse's company. If he hadn't convinced me in the first place that he wanted to talk about Flo, I wouldn't have gone with him. He never did discuss Flo. Such a boor." She looked at her plate. "I'm sorry. I forgot he's your boss."

"You're right. He is a boor." Hopefully Wallace would not be his boss for long. "And I'll only be there as long as necessary."

"What do you mean by that?"

In spite of his not wanting to sound like a blabbermouth, she had a way of getting him to talk. "Since I returned stateside, I've been trying to get a loan from the bank to start my own company."

Victoria's mother sat in the chair across from him. "I don't believe we've ever asked. What do you do, Joseph? I mean, I know you work for Wysse and Sons. What, exactly, does that entail?"

"Ma'am, I'm an engineer. Buildings. Overseas, I built temporary housing for the soldiers. I had thought, perhaps, with so many men returning, I could build small bungalows for the new families popping up all over."

Victoria looked up, curiosity washing her features. "Then why on earth are you working for the Wysse family? You should be working for yourself."

He didn't want to sound like a whining baby or that he deserved special consideration because he was a returning soldier. And yet she was right. He was doing all the wrong things. "Well, I planned on that, but it seems Mr. Flannigan wants more than a man's dreams and a handshake in order for him to justify a bank loan. I did explain that... Well, I don't want to worry you ladies with my problems."

Footsteps came up behind him. "Then why not worry me with them."

Joe turned. "Sir?" He stood to his feet and extended his hand. "Nice to see you again, Mr. Banks."

"Make this the last time I ask you to call me Art."

Joe mock-saluted. "Yessir, Art." He sat down and shifted his attention back to the huge wedge of chocolate cake Victoria's mother had served. He downed a sip of his coffee before digging back in. This house, these people. They made him feel at home, feel as if he belonged when he hadn't belonged anywhere in a long time.

"Mother, could you pour me a cup of coffee and cut me another slice of cake, too?" Art asked his wife. "If you ladies will excuse us for talking shop a moment, I'd like to hear what Flannigan told you, Joseph."

Joe swallowed over the lump of cake in his throat. "I—uh, well. Are you sure you want to hear all my woes, sir?" He'd rather finish the cake and leave. Like it or not, Victoria had managed to squeak through his defenses. He needed to leave. As soon as possible. If all he did was give her an occasional wave of the hand but keep walking on by, the better.

Art grabbed his plate. "I find that woes are best when shared, don't you think? Gives a man a chance to mull over the possibilities."

Victoria smiled at her father. Such a peach. Always trying to help other people. But she knew he didn't have extra capital to loan Joe. On numerous occasions when he didn't know she'd overheard, he told her mom that his own business had yet to get back on par with what it had been before the war. Less construction, fewer roofs to put up. So how did he think he could help Joe?

As Joe and her father talked about Joe's dreams for Howell, Victoria couldn't help noticing the way his hair had grown out since she first ran into him in Lansing. Now, with it thick and full, he had to keep pushing a lock from his forehead each time he leaned forward to take a bite of cake. When he glanced up, his eyes, dark brown with thick lashes, stared at her, their smile inching into her heart. Had he been this good-looking as a boy? She didn't remember him being so downright handsome. Gawky and gangly with big clomping feet stuck with her. But he was certainly attractive now.

Her father lowered his voice. "Well, Joe? What do you think?"

"Sir?"

Her father glanced first at Joe, then at her. He grinned. "Guess your mind was elsewhere."

Victoria's face fanned with red, she could feel heat reach all the way to her neck.

With a scrape of her chair, she stood to her feet. Joe and her father followed. "Let's do up these dishes, Mom, and give the men a chance to talk." *And give me a chance to recover from his attention.*

Though she busied herself at the sink, she heard every word between them.

"Joe, what kind of proposition did you make banker Flannigan, if you don't mind my asking?"

"Well, sir, I have quite a bit in savings, but the extra loan would go a long way to getting the company rolling right away. Nothing fancy, mind you. All I wanted was a modest building to work from—a place to plop my hat and roll up my sleeves. I wanted enough money to be sure I'd make payroll once the company grew. I had hoped to hire two men right up front. And they'll need room for tools, meetings with clients and a small space to call home away from home."

"And what type of structures?"

"Now that the war's over, I thought about building some nice little two- and three-bedroom bungalows for fellas returning, ready to start families. Nothing fancy, you see, just decent homes to raise a family in. Nearly every fellow I served with talked about nothing else as we built the temporary housing for them. Every man deserves a house of his own, don't you agree?"

"I do."

"And it isn't as if I have to prove myself as a worker. Mr. Wysse, the father, would no doubt speak well of my work ethic. I don't mind saying, the son isn't much when it comes to ambition, only at bossing folks around. In my mind, that's no way to run a business."

Art shrugged. "Never has been, son. Men respect what they see, not what they hear."

"I agree. Workers will give you all they have when they see you working alongside them. I'm a worker at heart, sir, engineer and all. I had hoped to buy Mr. Wysse out, but as soon as I suggested it, suddenly the oldest son wanted to be an active part of the family business. I'm still not exactly sure why. He has no ability and no inclination to see the business grow. If anything, I predict it will steadily decline once the old fellow steps down."

"And did you truly only offer a handshake and a smile to Flannigan?"

"No, sir. I offered to mortgage my house. Well, my parents' old house. It's mine now. But I was happy to use it as collateral. He still said no."

Her father cleared his throat. "I'm thinking I might have a solution."

"*You* have a solution…to *my* problem?"

Her father's words were tempered with kindness as he spelled out a plan.

With a purpose in his steps, Joe pressed through the wood-and-glass door that led directly to Mr. Wysse's office. As he slid around the son, Joe smiled and gave a small salute. "Wallace."

"Mr. Wysse to you." Wallace's eyes sparked outrage. Joe had no doubt Wysse was still fuming about last night whether he'd ever admit it or not.

"Good morning to you, too." Joe's grin couldn't hide behind the courage he had for this appointment. No more would he scrape and bow to Wallace Wysse.

"You'd better get to work, Huntington."

Again, Joe smiled. "Soon as I've talked with your father." And he immediately entered the elder Wysse's office, closing the door in Wallace's face.

"Good morning, Mr. Wysse. I appreciate your seeing me on such short notice."

"Sit down, m'boy. Good to see you. Hope we haven't been working you too hard."

Joe shifted in his seat. He hated this part, having to tell Mr. Wysse that it was time to move on. Wysse had been nothing but all wool and a yard wide, as his grandfather used to say. "Well, sir, that's why I'm here this morning."

"Beg pardon?"

"I've come to give you my notice. I'll be moving on in two weeks."

The elder Wysse tugged the gnawed cigar from his mouth and stubbed it into a silver tray next to the phone. "Leave? Why would you want to leave us? We pay you well, don't we?"

"Yessir. But I've always wanted my own company and I feel like now's the time to make my move." He stood and stuck his hand out. "I appreciate you giving me this job when I returned, sir. But I think I can make things happen to get my own business started. With all the returning soldiers, there's a need for my sort of company. Modest homes for young families. I'm excited to get started. I can't thank you enough for all your kindness."

Wysse pumped Joe's hand but didn't let go. "You'll be sorely missed, m'boy." His face clouded and he eyed the nasty cigar in the ashtray. The smell alone nauseated Joe. "Sorely missed. Nothing I can do to change your mind? A few extra perks to make the job more palatable?"

"I'm afraid not, sir." Was he thinking what Joe was thinking? That if the old man had to depend on Wallace to run the company, there wouldn't be a Wysse and Sons in a few months. "I'll keep my eyes open for anyone looking for work, sir."

Wysse clapped his other hand on top of Joe's, then dropped his hands to his sides at last. "Appreciate it, son. I'll ask Melinda to have your final check ready for you when the time comes. And, Joseph, there might be a small thank-you included for all the extra hours you've worked 'off' the company time, if you get my drift. You might think I didn't notice, but I did. You worked nearly as many hours off the clock as on." His head dipped to his chest, just for a second, and then he assumed the strained smile once more. "I do know what you've meant to the business. I appreciate it."

"Thank you, sir." While Joe was grateful, he thought it odd that on the surface, at least, Wysse's company didn't want for finances. Seemed the war hadn't hurt them at all. Were they seriously that solid in the industry with Wallace Wysse Jr. now at the helm?

Nonetheless, he wouldn't look a gift horse in the mouth. With that money and what he had saved, Joe figured he'd be able to put some capital into the new joint venture with Banks, even though Art had said it wasn't necessary at the moment. They could share work space and potential clients. Still, Joe wasn't dense. He knew the war had stunted all parts of the building industry and it was only beginning to recover. Art could use the extra money.

Victoria spun in circles as the little ones clapped. "More. More."

But her chest heaved as she flew through the added pirouettes. *Have to sit down.* "Whew, no more today, ladies. I'm afraid I'm a wee bit tired trying to keep up with you."

"Tired?"

"Of us?"

"No, not tired *of* you, but because I've been chasing you around."

They giggled and laughed, half of their smiles missing front teeth. Victoria placed a hand over her chest and grinned at the silly faces. "You're all dismissed for the day." And with that, she plunked onto the bench as the children scurried in all directions. Where did they get that kind of energy?

Her mind wandered to what Joe might be doing at the moment. He and her father had come up with some wonderful ideas to benefit both of them at work. Would that mean she'd be seeing more of Joe or less? Or not at all? She couldn't decide yet. Because the last thing she wanted was for them to feel awkward around one another.

"Victoria!" Flo's voice pierced the juvenile chattering.

"In here," she said, rising from the bench. "What has you all excited?"

Flo's face flushed pink. "I understand that nice Joseph Huntington is finally putting down roots in Howell. Is that right? He's going into business with your father?"

That nice Joseph? Had Florence set her cap for him? "Yes, he and my father *are* planning to work together. He can use Dad on projects, and Joe can help him to create new work for the company. But they're still trying to work through the logistics. I'd say it means he's going to be sticking around."

Again with the pink-tinged cheeks, Flo asked, "Are you and Joseph...I mean, are you two seeing each other? Or anything?"

"Not at all." Well, they weren't. She'd like it if they were, but Flo was her best friend. How could she say there was something between them when there wasn't? Just because he and her father worked together now didn't mean she and Joseph would be any more to each other than friends. At least that was something positive.

"I know the two of you have seen each other. You know, as in dating. Is it serious?"

"No, and we haven't been dating. But why would that matter?" Hopefully Flo wasn't intending to pursue Joe. If anyone wanted him, it was Victoria. She'd love to have Old Brown Eyes wink at her. But she had to be very careful what she said so Florence wouldn't be hurt.

"Oh, never mind. I just wondered. I saw him make eyes at you and I was hoping his flirting had been a passing fancy."

Always searching for the right man. With prayer and confidence, Flo would meet the right man in time. Victoria laid a hand on Florence's arm. "Flo, give it time. The right man is going to cross your path, in God's timing. Don't be in a hurry to hook yourself to the first guy who pays you a compliment. You're better than that. And whether it's Joe or somebody else, be sure it's what God wants for your life."

"It's easy for you to say, Victoria. You've always had beaus. Men buzz around you like the proverbial bees to honey. I'm not pretty like you."

What? Her best friend had no sense of confidence in herself. "You're right, Flo. You aren't pretty."

"I beg your pardon?"

"You're beautiful. Inside and out. You always have been, and when that right man comes along…well… he'll see it, too." *Just please don't let it be Joe.* Victoria didn't seem to be able to stop this growing attraction she had toward him.

Flo inched forward, wrapped Victoria in her arms. "You are the best friend a girl could have. What would I do without you?"

"The question is, what would *I* do without *you?*" She pressed out of Flo's hold and slumped back onto the bench. "You saw me through mountains of tears when I got a hope chest instead of a mitt. You carried baseball bats like a batboy even though you didn't play. You even put ice on my toes after Joe stepped on my feet at dance class. You've always been there for me, Flo. You're the true friend."

Florence's face flashed pink and she dipped her head in her humble manner. "I guess we're the sisters we never had. I only wish I'd spent more time in sports, like you. All those beautiful summer days when I locked myself inside learning to knit and crochet. I didn't meet a lot of boys that way, did I?"

"Well, that's in the past." Victoria sucked in a deep

breath, but nothing worked. The shortness of breath she'd had her entire life suddenly worsened.

"Flo?"

"I'm right here. What's wrong?"

"I...my..."

"Victoria!"

Her eyes...spots...the room spinning. Her fingers clutched at her chest, tighter and tighter as black spots filled her vision. What was happening?

She gasped, her mouth opening and closing for air. "I...Flo...Florence?"

Chapter 7

Dr. Cleewell towered over Victoria, his thick, outdated moustache twitching at the edges. "You frightened us, young lady."

"What happened?" She'd been talking with Flo, hadn't she? That was all Victoria remembered. That and the black spots before her eyes.

"I'm afraid you passed out at that dance school of yours. Florence drove you home and your folks called me right away. Gave us all a bit of a scare." He patted her hand, this doctor who had delivered her as a baby. She thought through her day, what she'd done, what she'd eaten. Nothing that should have caused her to faint.

"How about if you tell me what happened just before you passed out?"

"Nothing strange really. I'd finished with my young-

est students and was having a hard time catching my
breath. But that always happens right after class." And
she'd been thinking about that handsome Joe Huntington, but that shouldn't have made her faint.

Twitch…twitch. With a frown, he smoothed the ends
of the caterpillar of a mustache under his nose. "Always?"

"Certainly. When I was little it happened during and
after games, when I ran, you know? And it's been the
same with dance. Isn't that what happens if you run? I
mean doesn't everybody—"

"No, Victoria. Well, maybe now since I'm a bit older
than Methuselah, but not when I was your age. No, it
isn't what happens to healthy folks."

Healthy folks? She was healthy. Hardly sick a day
in her life. Dr. Cleewell was talking nonsense. He, of
all people, knew how healthy she was. "What are you
talking about?"

"Has this shortness of breath been getting worse?"

Had it?

"Or have you noticed anything else out of the ordinary?"

Getting worse…yes…yes, it had. But nothing she'd
be upset about. Too little sleep and too much bounc-
ing around in the classroom. Maybe a cold coming on.
"Now that you mention it, maybe a little. I've felt sort
of wobbly at times. Nothing really out of the ordinary.
But I suppose you could say I've been getting short of
breath more often than usual."

He sat on the edge of her bed, squeezed her hands in
his. "Now, it's important for you to tell me if this has
ever happened before."

"What do you mean happened before? It always happens."

Dr. Cleewell frowned at her and the mustache drooped toward the floor. Almost made her giggle in spite of his questions. "So you've had this feeling before? In fact, you say you've had it your whole life that you can remember? Just not this bad."

What kind of silliness was this? She was no different from anyone else. "Pretty much. At least as long as I can remember. Never stopped me from doing what I wanted any more than any other person I know."

"I'll bet it didn't. You have spunk, girlie."

"So what's wrong with me? Some cold or…something like that?"

"I have a few ideas. Just guesses, you know."

Stop guessing and spell it out. What was wrong with her? "And?"

Her mother pressed in, concern sprouting all over her normally calm face. "What? What do you think?"

He stroked his chin a time or two and glanced toward the door. "Will Mr. Banks be home soon?"

Victoria had had enough. Not a child any longer, she expected answers for herself. "Why is that important, Dr. Cleewell?"

"I thought, perhaps—"

"I don't mean to be rude, but I'm twenty-three years old, Dr. Cleewell. Old enough for good news or bad. And I'm assuming from the look on your face, you have bad news for me. So out with it, please."

He licked his lips, his gaze not wavering from the door. Finally, he looked her in the eye. "I don't know a hoot and a holler about hearts, Victoria. Not much, anyway, but I heard a faint murmur when I listened.

Instead of guessing, I'd like to send you to a specialist who should be able to get a handle about what's going on."

"But my classes!"

Dr. Cleewell's mustache flapped when he nearly shouted, "Classes? You're worried about classes at a time like this?"

The door opened and her father walked in. "Well, you've been waiting for Dad. You might as well tell him what you suspect."

"Benjamin, what's going on here?"

Victoria assured her mother nothing was wrong while her father spoke with the doctor. A lot of nonsense over nothing. Except her father kept gazing her way until she locked eyes with him, and then he'd look away.

"Well, Dr. Cleewell, when can I return to my classes?"

Her father stepped closer. "Victoria, this isn't any time to think about classes. Your health is what matters at the moment. We all want what's best for you. I have no doubt your girls will feel the same."

"Dad, I just overdid a bit. And the girls have been passing around a cold or something. I'm probably fighting that off. That's all there is to it."

"And this is what we want to find out…for certain. But there's no sense taking chances."

She looked beyond her father where Mom had gone to sit in the vanity chair, her eyes redder than a cherry. "Mom? Why, you're crying." This wasn't a cold. A slight heart murmur. No one cried over heart murmurs. What had Dr. Cleewell told her mother? And when? While she was passed out?

"Just concerned. I'm fine, dear."

But Victoria could tell there was more to this than she was saying. What was going on?

Joe had said he was stopping by to talk with her tonight. Not possible. "Mom, could you call Joe and tell him not to come tonight? Please?"

Her mother rose from the chair. "Of course, dear." But her gaze stuck on Victoria like glue to construction paper. She didn't want to leave the room.

"Thank you." Victoria waited a minute after her mother left and then turned to Dr. Cleewell. "Now, if you and my father will please tell me exactly what you think is going on."

Joe returned the phone to his desk. She had seemed fine this morning when he stopped in her studio. Must be coming down with something. Still…he should stop by and at least take the flowers he'd bought. No sense wasting a buck's worth of flowers.

A quick gaze around the front room and he reached for his coat. Why didn't he remember to hang it where it belonged?

As he climbed behind the wheel, he said an extra prayer that the old girl would start first try.

And she did!

The stars shone brighter than usual. Was that a good sign? Must be. His heart tripped when he thought of seeing Victoria, cold or no cold. Even with a red nose, she would be more beautiful than any other woman he knew. He imagined pulling her into his arms to protect her, to ward off any illness. Now, wasn't that silly? But he'd gladly try; any excuse to have her in his arms. Her head on his chest. The sweet smell in her hair that he remembered from the graduation dance. He closed his eyes and almost heard the music as his mind wandered back to the past.

With a reputation for not being able to dance, he did little more than a sad sway with the beauty in his arms. It didn't matter; merely holding Victoria meant the world to him. She looked up and locked her gaze with his, and he melted. Such a beauty. Sixteen years old, and the most beautiful girl in the world.

Then his happiness had popped like a bubble. Mrs. Pendergaster, the toughest chaperone, had quickly moved to their sides.

"Young man, you will keep a distance of one hand span between the two of you. You know better. We'll have none of that modern hanky-panky on our dance floor."

Joe stifled the chuckle. "Yes, ma'am. I guess I didn't notice."

"Didn't notice?" She adjusted the glasses on the end of her nose. "Humph. I'm watching you, young man. Do not think I'll allow any funny business." She meant it, too.

Now his empty arms ached to hold Victoria again. Closer, without Mrs. Pendergaster to interfere.

Joe looked up. No chaperone. No Victoria. Just his modest front room. Rose-colored wallpaper that his mother had hung after saving for years. The house was quiet, not alive the way it had been when his entire family filled the nooks and crannies. Loud voices, shouting boys, laughing parents. Now it was a lonely place. How he longed to fill it with joy again.

What had happened to his promise to himself that his business would be up and running before he found "the one" for him? He laughed. His promise hadn't taken into account reacquainting himself with blonde, blue-eyed Victoria Banks.

Since Art hadn't accepted any of his savings, assuring Joe he was bringing the expertise to the company, Joe might be able to swing getting married.

If she said yes. That is, if he got up the courage to ask.

There he went again, putting the cart before the horse. They hadn't even gone on a date thus far and already he was hearing wedding bells. But they had run into each other enough for him to know in his heart she was the only one. Or maybe he'd known that when she gave him a shiner ten years ago. Or when he picked her up for the dance almost seven years ago. She'd been waiting in a pale blue dress, the same color as her eyes. He'd bought a gardenia because the florist said it was the only flower to buy a special date. And she was special. Beautiful. Since then, any other girl he'd dated—and there'd only been a handful—had always looked like Victoria in his mind.

He shook his head. *Enough. She doesn't even know how I feel.*

Joe reached over and cranked the heat off. The car had suddenly grown very warm.

"No, Mother. I don't want him to see me like this. Please." Her words cut, and she knew it, but she didn't plan to have him see her looking like—like an invalid. If what she had was as serious a condition as Dr. Cleewell had intimated, more from his reactions than his words, then she had no intention of dragging Joe along. Maybe he and Flo might… She didn't want to think about that possibility right now.

Her mother struck a pose that broached no nonsense. "But, Victoria."

"No, I've made up my mind. And don't make that face, Mom. He's Daddy's work partner, nothing more. Now if you'd please turn out the light, I'll get some sleep. Dr. Cleewell said it's important I have plenty of rest until I go to Lansing."

"And that will be day after tomorrow, young lady. No piddling around, waiting. We want you to have the best care as soon as possible."

"Oh, Mom. Think of the costs. How will I pay the bills?"

Her mother closed the door gently, but Victoria heard the soft words. "We won't even think about that right now."

How could she not? And Joe? This could be very serious, in which case she had no intention of tethering him to a sickly woman.

There comes a time in anyone's life when being fair is more important than a handsome face.

In a sterile white ward with no other patients, Victoria shuddered when Dr. Quentin Weatherford marched into the room at St. Mary's in Lansing. All business, very professional. But cold. The look on his face worried her. Dr. Weatherford shook his head. He treated her like a child, addressing her father. "I'm sorry, Mr. Banks. I hear the murmur, and I have an idea from what she's told me what's likely to be going on, though it's quite uncommon in an adult of Victoria's age." He nibbled the edge of his lip and shook his head. "You need a cardiologist who deals with this specifically, not a man who tells old fellas who've indulged all their lives that they need to stop the riotous living. I'd recommend Dr. Gross in Boston. He's a pioneer in patent ductus arteriosus and the one who will be able to tell you for sure. I had the privilege of going to school with him, and there's none better."

Victoria caught the edge of his sleeve. "Talk to me, Dr. Weatherford. I am not a child. I want you to talk to me about what's wrong and what you think should be done."

Finally creased with compassion, his expression let on much more than his words had.

"It's that bad?"

He shook his head, patted her hand. "I can't give you a definitive answer. Though I plan on a few more tests here—"

"No, sir. They'll just repeat them in Boston. I'll owe my parents enough money as it is. No more tests until I get there. No sense paying for the same test twice. Because you intend to send me no matter what you find, is that correct?"

"Correct. Once you see Dr. Gross, I'll feel better if he says there's nothing wrong. But you need to consult with Gross. That is a given. He's the best there is."

"Thank you for your honesty. I'd like to speak with my father now, alone, please."

Her father put on a strained happy face, the kind a person wears when he wants to cry but must look happy. She was such a burden. When Dr. Weatherford left the room, she took her father's hand in hers. "Dad, this hospital alone is going to cost so much money. There's no way you can send me to Boston."

"We won't talk about money right now." He squeezed her fingers. "Not now. You are all that matters. We'll find the way. I can always mortgage the company."

"Oh, no, you don't."

Tears welled against the back of her lids and her lips trembled. How had she deserved parents like hers? She simply couldn't allow them to get in over their heads. Maybe if she just took it easy with the dance classes for a while. That was it; she just had to be more careful until she felt stronger.

"Dad, what if I simply take a break from the studi—"

"No what-ifs. You need to be seen by this special heart doctor, Gross. We want you well. Not patched together with tar and shingles. Fixed. Do you understand? And I won't take no for an answer. I'll make the arrangements tonight for your trip to Boston. A quick trip home to pack my own bag, and I'll return tomorrow to accompany you."

"Maybe if I go alone that would save us some money."

"Dr. Weatherford already put the kibosh on that. You have to go with an escort. And that is me."

Chapter 8

Art's rushing home from Lansing to return that same afternoon set everyone on edge. He had asked Joe to come over for a few last-minute instructions, and Joe walked in on him tossing clothes in a bag, unlike the organized man Joe knew him to be.

Joe sank into the oversize wing-back chair in the living room watching as he planted his hands on his knees and leaned forward. "What can I do to help?"

"Joe, I need you to hold down the fort while I'm gone." Art whispered to his wife, "And if you'd finish putting my shirts in the suitcase, I think I'll be all set for the train."

Mrs. Banks eyed the chaos. "I think that's wise." She refolded and smoothed the wrinkles from the top shirts in the suitcase, then fastened the clasp. Joe didn't miss the misty eyes that spoke of her desire to be the one going.

"I'm happy to do whatever you need, sir." Joe rose and lifted the suitcase. "If there's anything you need, ma'am, while he's away."

With Art's fingers steepled, he pointed at Joe. "Son, just your being available in a pinch will set my mind at rest. There's that new roof on the restaurant west of town."

"That's a huge project, sir. Won't they want you on-site?"

"I have no doubt of that, but Ben Harcourt is the supervisor on the job. He'll do fine." Yet the worried look on his face said Art wasn't as sure as he let on. Nevertheless, Art clapped his hands together as if that scrubbed the worry lines from his face. It didn't. Joe knew from talking with him that this project might make or break the recovery of the business. Art had to be worried sick. What a time for the owner of the company to leave town.

Joe clasped Art's shoulder. "Listen, if you folks would agree, I could accompany Victoria to Boston." Just a word with her. He must find out if she was all right. She hadn't seen him before she left for Lansing, and now…this. Why hadn't she been willing to talk with him? He didn't understand. "Or I could accompany Mrs. Banks so she could go."

Maybe that wasn't playing fair, but he wanted to see Victoria, and he didn't miss the way Mrs. Banks's eyes lit up at the suggestion.

"Joe, Victoria said she doesn't want to see you. I don't begin to understand what's going through her head at the moment, but you'll have to respect her wishes. Just as we have to. Victoria isn't a child anymore. She knows her own mind."

Joe wished Victoria knew *his* mind. How he'd love

to wrap his arms around her and tell her nothing could touch her, harm her. He wouldn't allow it. If only she would give him a chance to show her.

"Will you at least take a letter to her when you go? I just...I want her to know I'm thinking of her." He wanted to hold her, kiss her, tell her everything was going to be fine, but she wouldn't give him the opportunity. What had changed? Certainly not the fact that she had an issue with her heart. It couldn't be that. Surely she didn't think he was so shallow that he'd allow an illness to change his feelings.

"Of course I'll take the letter. Can you get it ready right away? I'll be leaving in a couple hours."

"Thanks, Art." Joe was taking his leave to fetch the letters he'd been writing when he saw Mrs. Banks from the corner of his eye. "Watch out!"

Her mind no doubt on Victoria, Mrs. Banks tripped over the small ottoman in front of her, and Joe's warning came too late.

Lying in the hospital bed for hours, Victoria had more than enough time to worry. She had begun to tally in her head all the costs her father was incurring. With his company on less than solid ground of late, she worried her illness would put him completely out of business. Her thoughts swirling, the palpitations increased to the point it was difficult for her to breathe again. The nurse would rush in if she wasn't careful. Stop, slow down. Take it easy or the only costs her parents would have would be a coffin and burial. She bit the edge of her lip. No. Not this young. Try as she might, she couldn't stop her heart from doing whatever it wanted. Pounding in her chest, fluttering against her ribs, sending pessimistic messages to her brain that this was more serious than it was. Then again, how did she know one way or the other? Not even Dr. Weatherford was sure.

More important, all she could think of was how unfair this all was to her folks. As an only child, she was aware of the heartbreak she'd cause them if anything happened to her. *Think about other things, Victoria. Pleasant, happy things. Get your mind off yourself.*

She closed her eyes to rest, to clear her brain, but in no time at all, a face appeared. *That* face. Dark hair, cocoa-brown eyes and a smile that would melt even a starlet's heart. Grinning at her in a manner that made her question not seeing him before she left. He hadn't had those deep dimples when they were in high school, had he? Or had she forever thought of him as little Joey Huntington, even in high school, her head blocking him out when her heart found him so attractive? The flutterbudget her aunt accused her of being.

This way of thinking wasn't healthy.

She shook her head. Didn't work. His smile crept up on her, dimples and all, surprising her, and brought her joy in spite of herself. This was crazy. He was an incredible man and didn't need half a woman, a used-up female with nothing to offer. A has-been. A worthless girl with only medical bills to bring to a marriage. Who knew what this would end up costing? When she'd asked Dr. Weatherford, he'd simply smiled and patted her hand, told her not to worry about such things. But his words had been as empty as his smile, which told her worry was *all* she should be doing.

What would she be leaving behind? She hadn't made her mark yet. Or had she? In all honesty, she'd like to think she had made a great deal of her life even if it hadn't been pitching for the Peaches or Belles. Her little dancers were proof of all the time she poured into her work.

Her head hit the pillow, and tears burned her eyes and then found their way to her cheeks. She wiped them away, but they returned again and again, soaking her hands and the pillow. She wasn't done yet. Not yet. She wanted a family, her own little ballerinas and ballplayers. A husband who loved her. But that couldn't happen, not with a weak heart, and wasn't that what the doctors had implied?

How she longed to have Joe with her, but that wasn't going to happen. Even on the baseball diamond she'd been emphatic about fairness. Always fairness. She giggled momentarily through the tears. Okay, she might have waived that the one time she pitched the shiner.

Still, in the end, fairness was what mattered.

No matter how she wished things could be different, it wasn't fair to Joe to be tied to a dying horse. And she was dying. The expressions on her father's and the doctors' faces told her as much. Why did she even need to go to Boston? Surely no one could fix a bad artery, or whatever the thing was. A duct. An opening that hadn't closed when she was born. Was Dr. Weatherford correct in his diagnosis? Only after seeing this man, Dr. Gross, would she know for sure. So she'd wait until she had the final verdict. Or was that already in and she was merely going to New England Medical Center for sentencing? Gross might slam the gavel, giving her a death sentence.

"No! I'm not ready to go!" The fluttering in her chest again. Oh, why wouldn't it stop?

A nurse dashed into her room. "Are you all right?

Can I get you anything?" Then a caring smile. "Would you just like to talk, Ms. Banks?"

"No, no and no. Of course I'm not all right. Some doctor in Boston is going to tell me that I don't have long to live. Why would I be all right?"

"Oh, now, we don't know any such thing. Let me call Dr. Weatherford. Maybe he can answer more of your questions. Keep calm and I'll be right back." She dashed from the room a little too quickly.

Shortly, a visit from the doctor earned her more medication to relax. He didn't seem to understand, no matter what they gave her or told her, she didn't have the faith that they would be able to fix Humpty Dumpty. She was broken beyond repair. No way could some doctor in Boston fix this. They were talking about her heart, for crying out loud. Doctors couldn't fix hearts. Could they?

In no time at all, grogginess set in. Victoria fought to stay awake but finally succumbed to the medication. Was she dreaming or only groggy as she thought about the life she'd never have? A life with Joe. Babies, a home, a future. How could she think of a future with him when she didn't even know if she'd have a future... of any kind?

With Mrs. Banks stretched out on the sofa, Joe helped Art ease an ice bag onto her leg, which was already swollen and purple. They had called Dr. Cleewell, but he hadn't arrived yet.

Art fluffed a pillow and wedged it under her head. Her skin, pasty white as a turnip, blended into the pale pillow, but her spunk stayed true to form. "I'm...hurt, dear. Not dead. Please don't fuss."

"But you're in pain. I can see that."

She tried for a smile, but the edges tipped slightly, nothing else. Even Joe could tell the pain overwhelmed her. He went to the window, pulled back the heavy floral drapes and kept an eye out for the doc. He looked at Art. "Should I try and call again?"

"No, son. He'll be along. That old wreck of his doesn't go so fast anymore." Like Mrs. Banks, all Art could do was attempt a smile, but his attention was wholly on his wife.

An engine coughed out front and Joe sprinted for the door to let Cleewell in.

Black bag and all, Dr. Cleewell entered and soon had everything under control. "I'd like a closer look with a fluoroscope. We'll need to get her a bit more comfortable before we move her." He pulled a small vial and syringe from his bag.

"What's that you have?" Mrs. Banks pushed up on an elbow and winced, and Cleewell gently nudged her back onto the pillow.

"No arguments. Moving you is going to be quite uncomfortable, madam. I don't want you feeling every bump in the road."

"But I must help...Arthur. His trip."

"What trip?" Cleewell's hand dove immediately for his hips, his gaze leveled at poor Art, who hadn't said a thing.

"Victoria." Art's eyes took on the worry Joe had seen in them earlier. "She leaves for Boston tomorrow."

Mrs. Banks added, "She can't go alone." Her words were strained and tight. She needed the pain medication badly. "I won't have my daughter going through this alone. Let's be straight on that."

Dr. Cleewell's attitude gentled. "I understand, but, Arthur, you can't leave your wife alone right now. Perhaps that flibbertigibbet friend of Victoria's. Florence?"

Her face a mask of pain, still Mrs. Banks said, "She works at the five-and-dime. She'd have to give…them notice. Ooh, this really hurts. Sorry to be such…a baby."

With a quick fill of the syringe, Dr. Cleewell redirected his attention to this patient. "Joseph, if you could step out a moment." Art appeared ready to pass out himself as the doctor made ready to inject his wife.

When Joe entered later with coffee for both of the men, Mrs. Banks's eyes whirled a second, her lids fluttered and she sank into peace. At least, Joe hoped it was peaceful. He hadn't ever taken more than an aspirin, but he'd seen drugs come in very handy in the war zone.

"There, now. She'll be much better." Dr. Cleewell asked to use the phone in the kitchen. "I have Mrs. Brady in labor and don't want to leave her in Jacob's hands for long. I'll let them know I'm on my way. Then, once Mrs. Banks is comfortable, I'll be back and we can move her to the clinic."

Art plopped into the heavy wing-back chair, his gaze never leaving his wife. "Joseph, I guess we'll have to take you up on your offer."

"Sir?"

"To accompany Victoria to Boston. Florence would no doubt take the time even if it meant being fired from her job, but I can't imagine a young woman could be ready as quickly as you could."

"A few seconds to throw a few clothes in a bag, and—"

"That's about all you'll have, son. The train leaves in a little over an hour now. Are you sure?"

A soft snorelike groan emanated from Mrs. Banks, and Joe smiled. "You have your hands full here, sir. I don't see how you could go even if you wanted to."

"Make no mistake, I want to. Very much. But I can't leave Mother like this. Folks might not talk, but I wouldn't forgive myself. Once I know she's all right, I'll have Mrs. Evans from church in to take care of her. Then I'll head for Boston."

Joe's mind swirled. He'd have to get a ticket and make arrangements for a hotel for tonight in Lansing and then in Boston. If the bank was still open, he'd need some cash for the trip. A million things to do. "Then, I suppose I'd better get a move on."

"Where's my head?" Art reached into his coat pocket. "Here you go. The ticket to Lansing and the tickets to Boston." He shoved an envelope toward Joe.

"Thank you, sir."

"No thanks about it. You're doing us a favor, son."

"I just wanted to help you and the missus out."

"You are helping us." He snapped his fingers and withdrew another envelope, a fatter one this time. "Also, I have a hotel booked for one night in Lansing. In Boston, your stay is for as long as you need. It will be at the Family Shamrock, an older hotel on Albany right near the medical center. A friend owns it, so you just have to put everything on a tab there. A couple of days later when I arrive, I'll take care of it all." He pushed the envelope into Joe's hand.

"Then I suppose I should get crackin'."

Art pumped his arm like an old water pump. Leaning on others didn't come easy for Mr. Banks, Joe could tell. So he left well enough alone.

Dr. Cleewell returned. "Now that she's out, let me

explain a few things. If this is a clean break, I might be able to set it in the clinic once I have a look. If not, she might be sharing a room with Victoria in Lansing." He smacked Art in the shoulder. "Don't worry. I didn't see anything that made me think I can't do it here. But she's going to need help for quite a while."

Joe and Art exchanged glances. Joe said, "As long as you need, sir."

"Joseph, you're a lifesaver."

Under his breath, Joe mumbled, "I only hope Victoria feels the same when she sees me instead of you, sir."

Sitting at the nurses' station, phone in hand, Nurse Lewis eyeing her every move as if she were a porcelain doll about to break, Victoria spoke as quietly as she could. "Oh, Dad, I'm so sorry. Poor Mom. Is she in much pain?" She pictured her mother pale and hurting, but not complaining one smidge. That was her way. Was that who Victoria had gotten her "spunk" from, as Daddy called it? Well, she'd show spunk now, as well. Didn't want either of them worrying she couldn't take care of herself. Dad should concentrate on no one but her mother.

"None to speak of at the moment, but the doc says when she comes around and that cast starts to squeeze her leg, she isn't going to be any too happy. I guess he'll be filling her with pain medication for the first few days. Tonight, for sure. He's keeping her at the clinic where he and Nancy Collins can keep an eye on her. Not that I plan on going home without her."

That was her father. He'd be right by Mom's side all night, holding her hand, patting her head, telling her how important she was and to get better fast. He was such a great husband. Always there to protect his beautiful wife. "Well, I understand. And I don't want you worrying. I'll be fine. I can certainly travel alone on a train." One way or the other she had to go to Boston and take whatever they handed out with good grace...alone.

"But you don't have—"

"I'm sure women have traveled to hospitals before without an escort. I won't be the first. And I have no doubt I won't be the last. You're such a silly. Don't concern yourself with me right now." But she'd be nervous, all right. What if something should go wrong? What if the news... No, she wouldn't think about that right now. Her parents needed for her to deal with this on her own. And she would.

"Victoria, I've made arrangements."

"You needn't worry, Dad. I'll be all right. Really." Nurse Lewis gazed over her shoulder, and the narrow squint changed almost immediately to a smile.

A throat cleared behind her. "Of course you will."

Chapter 9

"This is foolishness. I can't believe my father sent *you,* of all people, to chaperone his twenty-three-year-old daughter as if she were a child. And I was very clear, Joseph. I did not want to see you right now."

He wanted to laugh. Both of the Banks women were feisty. Both wanted to take care of matters on their own. Yet, when he looked at the pallor in a face that should have been rosy, he realized how ill Victoria was. So laughter wasn't a consideration.

"Listen, your father talked to them at the hospital and they insisted you travel with someone. They might have said you could only go with a medical escort or by ambulance, but I believe Dr. Weatherford agreed for you to go with family. To help with expenses."

"Foolishness and nonsense. You aren't family!"

"You've got me there." He'd like to be. Without much

consideration to the contrary, he'd come to the realization that he would really like to be. Hang the idea of his own business. Whether or not he had to go crawling back to Wysse and Sons, if it helped Victoria, so be it. After all, Art's small company could go under. It was struggling even now. That was one of the reasons they'd thought working together might be good for both of them. This was an expensive trip and Joe had heard that the surgery could be over a thousand dollars. More, maybe, depending on all they had to do. And if that meant Joe would have to kowtow to Wallace to get back his job, he'd do it.

He wouldn't like it, but he'd do it. For her.

As she sat there looking like the child she denied being, he offered his hand. "I'm a fill-in. Victoria, I want to help you. Please let me."

Her eyes brimmed with tears and she gritted her teeth, brushed them away and glared at him. He'd had the enemy do it with less gusto.

Nurse Lewis made a rumbling in her throat and Victoria rose from the chair. "I'm sorry. You want your seat back. *And* the phone." She still clutched it, like a weapon if Joe guessed correctly. And he'd already been on the receiving end of her anger a few too many times. Of course, he was in the right place to be treated if he ended up with another black eye.

Joe cupped her elbow and steadied her; he snatched his suitcase with the other hand. With a polite smile to the nurse, he walked with Victoria toward her room. "I didn't mean to upset you."

"Oh, I'm not upset. I'm really angry."

He wasn't sure how to respond. "I didn't mean to

make you really angry." His lips tilted enough to hopefully coax a smile from her.

She did smile. A sad one, but a smile nonetheless. "Oh, Joe. If truth be told, I'm not mad at you, at Mom and Dad or even at the doctors. I'm angry that this is happening. I've prayed about it, but I feel like God's not listening."

"You know better than that. He simply isn't giving you the answer you want right now."

"Isn't *that* the truth? I'd hoped I'd get here and Dr. Weatherford would tell me it's all been a misunderstanding, but I can see that isn't the case. And don't worry. I'm not mad at God. I understand that things happen to folks. To all folks. I had just hoped I'd have better news."

Joe hurt so much right at the moment, he thought his heart had truly broken. He gazed into the beautiful blue eyes that had softened his heart years ago.

Now that lively girl, that self-assured woman had grown pale and unsteady. And there wasn't a thing he could do to help her get better. He was almost upset to see her give in so easily. That didn't sit well. She never gave up, but here and now she was turning herself over to the situation far too effortlessly as if she had no fight left.

What could he do to change all this? He could pray, harder than he'd ever prayed before, hoping for a different answer this time just as she hoped.

"We'll take everything one day at a time. Let's pray for this Dr. Gross to really be the miracle man everyone says he is."

"There's only one real miracle man, Joe."

He smiled again. "You're right. And that's who we'll put our trust in. Okay?"

As he settled her into the chair next to the bed, she glanced at the bag in his hand. "You haven't checked into your room yet? It's getting late. You won't even be able to find a place to eat if you wait much longer."

Food didn't matter. The only thing that could nourish him now would be for her to get better. If only he dared hold her in his arms, let her feel his concern and protection. Well, at least she was talking to him, not angry anymore. For that, he was grateful.

Then, as if she could read his mind and didn't want him getting the wrong impression, she said, "I'm really tired. You'd better go. I'll be ready by eight." This time, there wasn't even a hint of a smile. She rose and sat on the edge of the bed, her flannel robe barely reaching her toes.

He grabbed for the blanket at the end of the bed and covered her legs.

"I'll get that." Her words sounded as if she was ready to burst into tears. "No need for you to wait on me and worry."

Not worry? She might as well have told him not to breathe.

For a while there, Victoria had nearly let the wall fall down. Had almost decided Joe was up to the task of facing whatever was wrong with her. But sentencing him to a life of servitude to a woman who couldn't give him a family, a home, only a sickly wife, wasn't the right thing to do. Victoria knew that better than most. She had seen her uncle Jack take care of her aunt for fifteen years before Aunt Edith finally passed away, a withered, broken shell of a woman.

Father's youngest sister, Edith, had fallen ill with

scarlet fever on her honeymoon. No one thought she would survive, but after three months of constant nursing, she'd come through the worst of it. Still, she hadn't been right after that. As a child, Victoria had overheard her mother mention once to her father that she thought *the fever* had affected Aunt Edith's heart.

Her heart. Victoria shuddered. She'd had some high fevers as a child. Could it have been that? Surely not. Doctors knew all about high fevers. None of them had suggested that might have caused her problem.

Aunt Edith hadn't been allowed to have children, so she and Uncle Jack grew old and alone together. With Aunt Edith in bed much of the time.

No one came right out and said for sure what was wrong and children weren't allowed to ask such things, but Victoria understood now just how much Uncle Jack had given up in life for his darling Edith. He had tended to her every need each night when he came in from work.

Victoria recalled one instance when Aunt Edith had taken so much time in the kitchen just to get tea into the cups for her visitors, and how she had to sit right away in a special chair to catch her breath, her legs covered with a lap robe. She'd wanted to do a lot more things; her mother explained to Victoria she simply couldn't. What a life, sitting in a chair most of the time. What had she done all day when there were no visitors? Stared at the wall until Uncle Jack came home? Read books? Maybe she knitted; Victoria did remember getting a pretty scarf from them one Christmas. Would that be enough for Victoria…knitting?

Would she even be well enough to do that? What if this Dr. Gross had no reason to believe he could repair her heart? What if she sat in a chair the rest of *her* life with a lap robe on her legs? When Joe had covered her feet, that was all she'd thought at that moment. It was why she'd told him it was time to leave.

Victoria was not about to allow Joe to come home to a sickly wife each night. No chance of a…real life together. No children. Her face warmed. She rubbed her cheeks. Silly to be foolish about it when she didn't yet know all that her illness entailed.

The truth was, she understood the birds and bees enough to realize that if her heart was bad they couldn't…have the family she wanted. No. If she allowed Joe to creep one more inch into her heart, she wouldn't be able to let go, and this wasn't any kind of life for a strong, strapping man like Joseph. A man who would want a whole wife.

She fell against her pillow, tears pooling for what must have been the dozenth time in the last forty-eight hours. Then she pulled the pillow to her chest and punched it. Punched it hard. She had to make a difficult stand. Tomorrow. Tomorrow Joe had to realize they could just be friends and only as long as it took for her father to get to Boston. After that there was no reason whatsoever why he should see her again.

Before the sun could ease through the boring brown curtains of his hotel room, Joe fitfully rolled over in bed as he had done all night. Not sleeping, not really awake. Caught between sleep and fear. Fear for Victoria and what this trip might mean for her future.

He plumped the pillow and closed his eyes again. Five more minutes and then he'd give up if he didn't doze off. With closed eyes, all he saw was a smiling face. More alive than a newborn. More beautiful than nature. More desirous than his first chocolate malt. Now, that brought a smile to his face. Sitting up, he eased his arms over his head and stretched. He'd need every ounce of strength to convince her he would love her no matter the outcome in Boston. That is, if he ever got the courage to tell her in the first place.

Didn't she realize that if he had to hold her in his arms every day without reward to keep her safe, to keep her happy and content, then so be it. He loved her that much.

He pulled back the matching dull brown quilt and jumped from the bed, wasting no more time. A quick wash up and he'd head for the hospital. Maybe he'd have a chance to talk seriously with Victoria before they caught a cab to the train station.

A knock on his door caught him before he grabbed his jacket.

"There's a call for you downstairs, sir. A Mr. Banks?"

Joe dropped a coin in the boy's hand and sprinted for the stairs.

The clerk held the phone aloft and motioned for Joe to step behind the counter. He dropped into a chair offered, and the other man stepped away.

"Art? What's going on?"

"Well, I shouldn't worry you about it, but to be honest…can you hear me all right, son?"

"Yessir."

"Must be scratchy on my end. Well, then. Good thing you thought I should stay behind. Supervisor called me and said the roof job's not going forward. He arrived at the site this morning and found the owner there. Owner told him that the bank withdrew the funds. That's all I know for now, but guess I'll be spending the day trying to right the problem. I just wanted you to be aware I'll be out and away from the phone. And I don't want Mother getting any upsetting news with me not home. So if you could wait till later in the evening whenever you call us, I'd appreciate that. Reverse the charges, of course."

"Art, I doubt we'll know much before we leave this morning."

"I know, but just in case. Mother is full of pain medication and I don't want her worrying. Cleewell is sending her home later this morning with the lady from church to watch over her. I'll try to fix this mess, and then I'll be home to take over. I don't want you worrying, Joseph. Just take care of our girl."

Joe thanked the clerk and dashed up the stairs to get his coat. Why on earth would the banker stop a loan to the restaurant owner? From what Art had said, the man's business was doing very well. This was one of the first really big commercial agreements Art had contracted. Wysse usually landed the commercial work and Art the residential. This would have been a great chance for them to grow in Howell. So strange. The restaurant owner had been adamant that Art get the bid and they had been ready to go forward.

When might the Banks family have a little good news for a change?

Joe hefted the suitcase Victoria had ready and waiting onto the bed. "So, you have everything packed?" He couldn't help noticing her sweater hung on her a bit. Had she lost weight that quickly? He hated this not knowing.

"All ready."

The morning nurse, Mrs. Siek, plastered on what

was probably a well-practiced smile for patients facing the unknown. "We'll miss this girl." She spoke to Joe. "She's going to be just fine." Then she turned to Victoria with an envelope in her hand. "These are to go to Hospital Admitting. Be sure they get it and put the paperwork into your chart. Dr. Weatherford's number is on there if they want to speak with him. And there's one more paper for you to sign before you leave."

Joe had watched her sign two sheets already. How many more were there?

Siek laid a hand on his arm. "Why don't you take your bag and her suitcase down to the front and hail a cab? I'll bring Ms. Banks out." She stepped into the hallway for a second and returned with a wheelchair.

Victoria's face fell…hard. "I have to go in a wheelchair?"

"Yes, ma'am. Hospital policy." Siek still had the same smile, only Joe noticed it didn't reach her eyes. To him, it festered on her face like a sore. Healing but painful. Did she put on such a show for all her patients? Of course she must. It was part of the job to always appear optimistic and happy.

Victoria looked as lost as Joe had ever seen her. He grabbed his coat from his shoulders and started to drape it over her legs before he went for the cab.

Her face warned him off before she shouted, "Stop that!"

Chapter 10

Joe and Victoria left the South Station and stopped only long enough for Joe to register at the Shamrock and leave his bag. Victoria waited in the cab, wishing the cabbie would crank up the heat some. The two-and-a-half-day train ride had been unbearable. After screaming at Joe at the hospital, she had barely spoken to him on the trip to Boston, too ashamed of her behavior to broach the subject. She'd been raised better than that. And no amount of self-pity permitted this kind of attitude. After all, it wasn't Joe's fault she was ill. It was no one's fault. It was just the way it was.

Maybe it was for the best. This way she wouldn't even need to bring up the friend issue she had decided on.

Joe slid into the front without looking over his shoulder. "New England Medical Center, please."

She didn't miss how tight his jaw was, pulsing with each word. He was beyond angry. He was downright mad. At her. Had been the entire trip. Well, what did she expect? She had treated him very poorly on the train. Hours and hours of no talking until it was time to grab a pillow and catch some shut-eye. Then it started all over again the next day. They had barely spoken at stops or when they shared meals. Only enough to say *pass the salt please* or *could I have the ketchup?* Victoria stifled a scream. She longed to yell how unfair all of this was to her, to Joe, to her parents. She thought she'd dealt with these feelings already, but apparently not. She still included whining in her prayers each night, but God didn't seem to mind or to be listening at the moment.

The flutters in her chest and the shortness of breath hadn't eased up for a second.

Victoria chewed the edge of her lip the way she used to do when pitching. A habit her mother tried her best to keep her from. "Thank you for accompanying me to the hospital, Joe."

He gazed straight ahead. "You're welcome. I promised your father."

The cabbie's head turned slightly when Joe spoke; then he looked into the rearview mirror. "And a promise to a father is a promise, miss."

Joe raised his eyebrows. "Thanks. I can speak for myself."

The cabbie replaced his smile with a scowl and looked straight ahead.

"Sorry—" Victoria sighed "—that this trip has inconvenienced you. I doubt my father would have wanted that. I know I don't."

She slunk farther into the seat. She couldn't even find a reason to get upset. His aloofness was well deserved even if the timing did seem poor at best. The cabbie looked as if someone had slapped him for trying to be nice.

"Well, thank you anyway." She gazed at the driver in the rearview mirror. "And thank you." He nodded but kept his eyes on the road ahead.

Sooner than expected, they stopped. Joe tipped the driver, extra if Victoria saw correctly, no doubt feeling guilty for his rudeness. Then he strode to the back of the cab. If she'd had the ability to sprint out the door, she would have. Instead she waited patiently for Joe to get out the suitcase. The cabbie opened the door for her, his smile back in place. "Miss?"

The building was huge. No wonder amazing medicine happened here. She hadn't seen anything like it before.

Would Dr. Gross come over from Children's Hospital today, or would they get her settled first?

Whatever the hospital decided, she was sure Joe would leave as soon as he could, pleasing them both. He'd barely said a word to her.

This time, an orderly rolled out the wheelchair and met her at the curb. Her insides withered like a vine. No sense fighting it any longer. She climbed in, no questions asked this time.

Joe steadied the suitcase and strolled along behind Victoria and the orderly. As soon as they entered, he gave a nod to the fabulous facility. A far cry from Dr. Cleewell's clinic, though Joe couldn't complain. Cleewell did a great job for the citizens of Howell. In spite of the fact that the clinic was housed in one of the older residential buildings in Howell. A three-story brick mansion that had been donated to Cleewell when Mr.

Millberg, one of the past mayors, had passed away. Cleewell made great use of it. Old house or modern facility, Joe hated hospitals and all they represented.

A clang startled Victoria. Joe glimpsed a rolling cart with metal bedpans on it; one had fallen, making all the noise. The orderly shouted, "Way to go, Biggs. Good thing they were empty." A quick frown from the guard in the front brought an end to that exchange.

Following the signs, they were directed to Admissions. A woman in a black dress who sported severe gray waves motioned for him to enter. "Who are you bringing in, sir?"

"Victoria Banks."

"Oh, yes. We've been expecting you folks. Are you the one who will be making arrangements for Mrs. Banks, sir?"

"Yes, ma'am. Here's the paperwork from Dr. Weatherford in Lansing." Did she say Mrs.?

"Thank you. And you'll be the one responsible for your wife's...expenses?"

Victoria didn't seem to catch that. She'd have plenty to say if she had. No doubt making it very clear Joe wasn't her husband, wasn't her anything. "Not my wife. She's a friend, but yes, I'll be making those arrangements. May we get her settled first?" Then the woman eyed him warily. He was making a mess of things. "Her mother is ill and neither of her parents could come along. I work with her father and am a friend of the family. It fell to me to bring her."

Victoria's head snapped up and her gaze narrowed on him. He guessed he'd said the wrong thing...again.

"Ma'am. She's very tired. Maybe the gentleman could take her to her room."

"Very well." To the young man, she raised her eyebrows. "Two fourteen. And don't dillydally." Despite the slight frown to the orderly, she immediately replaced it with a smile for Victoria. Must have been an expression she repeated quite often. Once they left, she addressed Joe. "Of course. She'll be fine with James while you and I talk. We should take care of matters right away. That way there won't be any misunderstandings."

Joe raised his voice slightly so Victoria could hear. "I'll bring your suitcase when I come up."

She didn't look back, just murmured, "Fine."

The woman held out her hand. "My name is Mrs. Mapes. If you'd come this way."

Joe followed her to a small desk. "We expect Ms. Banks will be here at the very least for three days. I prepared this ahead of time so you'd have an idea of costs. This is the amount for three days' stay." She pushed a paper toward him with dozens of items listed. "That will have to be paid before the doctor comes in. Once he begins tests, we'll have a better understanding of what the expenses will be. I'll consult with you on a daily basis. That should work fine, don't you think, Mr....?"

"Joseph." No, she was all business. No sense pretending otherwise. "Mr. Huntington will be fine." She seemed pleased that he returned a sense of formality.

"Mr. Huntington, we can take a check or cash. Would you like a minute?"

"Thank you."

She stepped out and he was glad. Didn't want her to see him scrounging through his wallet.

He drew the envelope from his pocket and counted out the amount she had quoted him from the cash he had left. No problem. Art had included enough for twice that many days. But he did have cabs back and forth. It was such a short distance, maybe he'd walk and try to save some more of the money.

Turning in his chair, he searched for Mrs. Mapes. She made eye contact with that painted-on half smile and returned to the desk.

"Here you are, Mrs. Mapes."

She accepted the money and passed him a receipt. All the while, Joe was concerned about Victoria. He wanted to sit with her, despite the uneasiness between them on the train ride. If only he could offer some peace, some calm to her. That's why he was here, after all. Staying angry over his hurt feelings didn't serve much purpose.

After asking for her room number again, he excused himself, but not without Mrs. Mapes donning a *look* that said there had better not be any funny business. Seemed to Joe that he rubbed older women the wrong way lately. He chuckled, remembering the grandmotherly woman at the recital who had given the impression she thought he was gaping at little girls. Did he have that kind of face? He sure hoped not.

Was Victoria sore at Joe again? She searched her soul and realized she wasn't sure. All things considered, he'd upended his life, put it on hold for her. He didn't have to do that. She could have traveled alone. It wasn't as if she was helpless, but no matter how much she argued with herself, in the end it sure felt good to have him beside her.

James gave her his arm and she switched from the wheelchair to the edge of the bed.

"Thank you." He wheeled the chair to the corner and pushed it out of the way.

"Anything I can get you before I leave?"

He'd been kindness itself. Perhaps everyone here would be the same. "No, thank you."

"All righty, then." He swung out the door, energy galore, and she was a smidge jealous. Oh, she didn't begrudge him his energy; she simply longed for some herself.

This wasn't a ward like in Lansing. This was a semi-private room. Her throat clogged again. More expense for her father. For her, once she started paying him back.

Thankful he had the huge restaurant job, she relaxed for a minute, remembering how he'd hopped around the kitchen, so out of character for him, when he landed the contract. He'd grabbed her mother and swung her through the air. "Things are looking up, Mother. Really looking up." Then he'd glanced at Victoria. "I just might be able to help you with the first month's rent on an apartment if that's still what you'd like to do. I know how cramped you feel living with Mom and Dad." He'd reached over and clipped her chin. "And you never complain."

So what? She'd have to live with her folks a little longer.

The room closed in. The white drapes, white blanket, white metal bed all mocked her. Purity, freshness, no blemishes. Not like her. Only one thing stood out. She stared at the wheelchair the orderly had left in the corner of her room.

This time, she choked back tears. If a wheelchair was the result of all this, she'd be living with her parents the rest of her life, or what there was of it. *Lord, please grant me some peace. I'm so afraid. If only...if only I knew what was going to happen. I've never felt this way before, Lord. Afraid, and I don't want to be a burden to anyone. Please let this Dr. Gross be the one to do Your good work. But if that good work is incomplete in any way, give me the strength to accept the outcome.* She eyed the chair again across the room.

Even if it means my worst fear.

Joe heaved a sigh. Art was worried. So was he. With a glance at the itemized statement Admissions had given him, his gut clenched. Not the kind of news he wanted to tell Art about. Not after what Art had divulged this morning. Once they had a handle on what Dr. Gross might do, he'd have another quote for the poor man. Couldn't be good, but financial arrangements would have to be made no doubt. That Mapes woman meant business. He understood it was her job. But did she have to be so good at it?

He folded the statement and put it in his coat pocket. Hopefully he'd be welcome when he arrived at room 214. They had told him earlier at Admissions that she would be going through some lengthy tests, so he needn't go up until after lunch.

After grabbing a coffee and a sad excuse for a sandwich, Joe headed up the stairs. The smells of the hospital soured his stomach. Antiseptic. Body odors. Chemicals of what nature he couldn't guess. The stairs even had a faint odor that let him know someone hadn't stopped in the restroom first. Bile rose and he swallowed hard to force it down along with the worst of his memories. The smells reminded him of the war, and memories of the deaths of his best friends, twins Jimmy and John Drake, grabbed him around the throat.

Joe's hand sought the stairway wall. He waited while his lunch settled and he forced the memories from him. He'd thought those recollections had been firmly shoved away where he didn't have to dwell on them anymore. Apparently not.

Now he remembered why he hated hospitals.

Chapter 11

After a full day and night of tests and now this disgusting lunch of tuna melt and warm milk, Victoria spent a few minutes placing a call to her parents to check on her mother. Anything to keep her mind away from what she would be facing shortly. The nurse had told her that Dr. Gross was coming in from Children's Hospital after his lunch hour, so she didn't have much time.

"Well, thank you for taking the call, Mrs. Evans. I just wanted to be sure Mom is all right."

"Fine, dear, fine. Dr. Cleewell has prescribed pain medication, so your mother is mostly sleeping. I'll let her know you called. And you take care of yourself."

Take care of herself? How was she supposed to do that?

She took her time returning to her room. At least the staff didn't rush to her side to force her into that stinking wheelchair. They had used it to transport her all over the hospital the day before when she'd endured one test after another. Now not having to sit in it helped her to feel a bit more in charge.

Yesterday had been hopeless. Prodding and pushing from an array of doctors and nurses all morning with no sign of Joe. Then when he did arrive, she'd been so tired and cross that not even his smile had broken through her unwelcome veneer. He'd left almost immediately with the excuse he probably had paperwork to fill out at his hotel. Paperwork? Sad excuse for *I've got to get out of here and fast.* As cross as she'd been, how could she blame him?

Now, looking out the window across from the nurses' station, she drew in a breath as a cardinal flew by. He stopped for a minute on the edge. He looked in, cocked his head and flew off in search of who knew what. Probably some female cardinal. That brought a tilt to her lips and sunshine to her day.

"That's quite the smile. I haven't seen you smile in days."

Drawn toward the familiar voice, and for no apparent reason, she didn't feel her usual irksome self. "That bird. Came right up to the window and peeked in at me. He was beautiful." So was Joe if she had to be honest. Beautiful, handsome, gorgeous, whatever she should a call a guy with searching eyes and lips that she longed to feel against hers. There had been two times when she imagined he wanted to kiss her. Why did she fight that temptation?

That's right…the fairness issue.

"He must not be afraid of people." He drew closer. "Are you afraid of people, Victoria?"

"Of course not."

"Of me?"

Without warning, he was getting too close to the truth. "Whatever do you mean? I'm not afraid of you."

"No?" He took another step toward her and she backed up, smacked into the window frame. "Then why do you keep pulling away from me? Every time I get close, those eyes of yours sprout hands and they push me far away. Why?"

Was that a smirk on his face? How dare he? She could back away all she wanted and what was it to him? With nowhere left to go, she dropped her gaze, nibbled her lip and forced the betraying thoughts from her head. "You have quite an imagination, I'm sure. No one's pushing you anywhere, Joseph."

"Joseph now, is it, Ms. Banks?"

"Oh, stop the foolishness, Joe. I need to go back to my room." But he continued to press in toward her, not even considering the nurse standing a few feet away.

As he inched closer, Victoria's heart took on the noise of a symphony, the drums rattling in her chest. He searched her face. "Are you all right? You're pale all of a sudden."

And you're teasing me. Stop it. I can't take this anymore. Had she said that out loud? *Go away...go...* Her legs wobbled and then the black spots again.

"We need help!" While Joe shouted over his shoulder, he didn't wait for anyone else. He snatched Victoria into his arms, searched the numbers on the wall and dove for her room, just steps away. He placed her on the first bed as he entered.

Some kind of bell rattled near the nurses' station and

after stuffing a pillow under Victoria's head, he stepped to the doorway. "In here. She fainted."

A nurse dashed to his side, her white hat nearly fluttering from her head. She grabbed it and said, "Sir, you'll have to step out." She pushed at him and drew a heavy curtain around the bed. As he backed out of the room, two other nurses and what looked like a doctor sprinted in, all of them talking at once:

"What happened?"

"Nothing really."

"No, one minute she was looking out the window, then talking to that gentleman in the hallway—"

"Then she collapsed."

"Was she upset? Did he say anything to bother her? Did she raise her voice?"

"Nothing, Dr. Benson. Nothing at all."

"She made a call to her home but was fine after that. Not upset at all."

"I called Gross. He's on his way."

Joe waited in the doorway until one of the nurses pushed past him. "You'll have to go to the waiting room at the end of the hall. Or downstairs. But stay out of the way."

She was back almost in an instant with a glass bottle and thin rubber hoses. "Let's move along, now."

He took one last look into the room. All he saw were feet below the curtain like stick people standing next to her bed. She needed more than stick people to save her.

Joe headed for the waiting room, where the silence nearly killed him. He had to know what was going on in room 214.

Hands clasped, he bowed his head. *This nightmare has to end, Lord. Give her a chance to live. A chance to fight. She's always been a fighter. Let her remember that.*

A man in a smart suit, dark hair, late thirties to early forties marched past the waiting room. In his hand, the usual black bag that Joe had grown to dislike because it meant illness. Still, the man walked with purpose and Joe followed his steps the whole way down the hall to Victoria's room. Then he realized it was the famous Dr. Gross. He'd seen him briefly the day before.

Joe followed along and stood outside the door despite what the nurse had told him.

"There we are, now. You gave us a scare, young woman. Remember me? Dr. Gross? Would you mind if I examine you again?" Then a "hmm" and an "aha" followed by "I'd like to see the test results."

A very weak voice murmured something that Joe didn't understand.

"How long have you felt weak and tired like this? You didn't mention this yesterday.

"No other warning signs?

"Just recently, then."

And the examination continued as the doctor verified one more time all that Victoria had told the other doctors back home. Joe stepped away when a nurse exited, but she was in such a hurry she didn't seem to notice him standing there this time.

Gross exited next. He stepped behind the nurses' station and seemed to be examining…tests? Joe couldn't be sure.

Then the doctor headed back to 214.

"Nothing to eat or drink after midnight. Let's have a look at this in the morning. Ms. Banks, I've looked over all your tests and I think we can fix you up just fine. Do you want an explanation of what I plan to do?" Then he laughed at something she must have said. "All right, then. We'll keep you calmly and comfortably in the dark until I get back later. I'll do a few more tests, and then tomorrow morning we should be ready to make you feel like a new woman. Nurse Malcome will go over the procedure with you later, as much or as little as you care to know. But there are a few things you need to be aware of so they don't surprise you after the operation."

The nurse returned with a syringe. Joe stopped her on her way back out of the room. "Will I be able to see her after Dr. Gross leaves?"

"I gave her something to relax her, help her sleep. I doubt she'll even know you're there."

"Then could I sit with her?"

The woman smiled and winked. "I suppose that would be all right."

Twenty minutes that felt like an hour passed, and the doctor left along with the nurses. The one he'd spoken to earlier stopped and patted his arm. "You can go in now, for a while. Try not to waken her. She needs the sleep."

Things were moving so fast. Joe thought the tests would take days. Was Victoria's condition that obvious? Why hadn't any of them seen a problem before? He had known her for years, and not in his worst imagination did he think she had a heart problem. Why now?

He stepped into the room and sat in the chair next to her bed. Her eyes fluttered for a second and then she appeared to be in deep sleep. "Victoria?"

Nothing. He reached for one of her hands. Soft, but so thin now. And with a needle in the back of her other hand, he traced the line to the glass bottle over her head, wondering what they were giving her.

"Honey, can you hear me?"

Her lips trembled for a second. Trying to talk? Her lips moved, but no words came out and she continued to sleep.

Joe stroked the back of her hand. "Victoria, I don't know if you can hear me or not, but I want you to know one thing. I love you. From the day I stepped on your foot for the first time until the shiner. Then when I picked you up for the dance, I couldn't believe my eyes. You were the most beautiful girl I'd ever seen. I thought I'd lost you after that and tried my best to drive you out of my heart. Other relationships, situations. But I don't think I did a very good job of it." His fingers curled around her hand, and instead of warmth, her hand was cool to the touch. He didn't like that one bit. He wrapped her hand completely in both of this, allowing his own body warmth to take the chill from her skin. He leaned in and kissed her fingers.

"Then when I saw you in Lansing, it all came flooding back. Your beauty, inside and out, the way you stand your ground, your spunk. And I wanted you in my life again. Still, I thought you lived in Lansing and figured I wouldn't ever see you."

Joe brushed the hair from her forehead. "And six months later, I watched you whirling around on your toes, dancing across the stage, and my heart melted. I guess that doesn't sound very manly or romantic, but it did. I haven't been the same since. My dearest Victoria, I'll love you until the day I die. I want you to be part of my life. I want us to grow very old together. You and me. Together forever."

He laid his head on the edge of the bed. If only she would wake up and let him pour his feelings out the way he wanted, but instead a throat cleared behind him. Startled, he whirled around. Mrs. Mapes and her patent frown.

This time, the oak desk in front of the matronly woman mocked him. Twice in two days. It felt like when he'd been sent to the principal's office again. Once for the tiny frog in Sissy Faith's soup, and the next time for glue on Mrs. Glasser's seat. How was he to know that glue would set up so quickly? And his father had to buy the poor woman a new dress. He sighed, remembering how hurt his father had been. That injured look had bothered Joe more than the two trips to the woodshed. Being paddled the second time had been eye-opening. He made sure that had been his last experience with a switch.

The look on Mapes's face, however, caused his hand to reach behind. He nearly rubbed his backside when she leveled a stare over her reading glasses and said, "There will be a matter of another payment, I'm afraid. Mr. Huntington, I realize you are here at the behest of Ms. Banks's father and mother. But this matter must be handled within the next few hours. I apologize. I had assumed we would have more time to work out the details, but Dr. Gross feels the need to do surgery right away. I'll need this amount before he will be allowed to start in the morning." She pressed another paper into his hands. "Your bill with him is his business, but we have to be sure the hospital will be paid in a timely manner. Within forty-eight hours is what we prefer."

"I—uh, I don't have that kind of money with me. Let me call Mr. Banks and—"

"I think that's wise. We will need half of this to proceed in the morning and the rest when we release Ms. Banks." She fiddled with the papers. "Unless, of course, Mr. Banks makes other arrangements."

Joe's forehead, now drenched in sweat, furrowed. He did his best to appear agreeable, but this was outrageous. How was he supposed to come up with this amount of money by morning?

He had no choice but to call Art. "May I use your phone? In private?"

"Of course." She stepped around the desk and headed toward the door. "You will be reversing the charges, of course?"

"Naturally."

A minute later his call was going through. "Thank you, operator. I'm waiting. Art? It's Joe. I'm glad I caught you in."

"No reason for me to be out anymore. I talked with Flannigan about the loan. He's the one who stopped the owner from going forward with the roof."

"You couldn't fix the problem?"

"No, son. Flannigan seemed downright unfriendly. I didn't notice that in the past. Why, we've enjoyed a great professional relationship through the years. Not thick as thieves or anything but good business partners. I don't get it. I really don't. At any rate, finances will be a bit tight until I can convince him to go ahead with the loan."

"Sorry to hear that."

"I suppose when the time comes, I'll have to speak with the finance department at the hospital. Arrange some sort of payments to cover Victoria's bill."

Joe's mind wandered. Was all of the tension because Joe had quit at Wysse's and decided to work with Art?

Surely Flannigan wouldn't want to stop them from a partnership. Joe thought Flannigan would be happy that Joe was *proving himself* more by working with a businessman who'd been strong in the community for years.

Then as plain as day, he remembered the photo over Flannigan's desk. Flannigan and Wysse, arms around each other's shoulder. Surely that didn't have to do with business. "Art, are Flannigan and Mr. Wysse very close?"

"Certainly. Wallace Wysse Sr. and Flannigan are in-laws. Why do you ask?"

Chapter 12

Joe slumped against the desk. Flannigan. He wasn't
going to help Art no matter what. Pure out-and-out con-
flict. And Joe was the cause. He knew Art had put all of
his savings into the company during the war to keep it
afloat, and now when he needed it…there wouldn't be
any left. Why hadn't he taken Joe's money when they
decided to work together? Now he'd have no choice.
He'd have to call information for the bank's number.

"No reason, sir. Let's get down to business. We need
to talk about Victoria. Gross is doing the surgery in the
morning. I have his number here. He said to call if you
had questions and I figured you would." He replaced
the receiver in the cradle.

Mapes would be back soon, and she would want answers. How could he fix the problem in time? Moisture
speckled his forehead in spite of how cool they kept the

hospital. He had to call his bank if Victoria was to have her operation in the morning.

Flannigan couldn't hold Joe's savings hostage, even if he had disrupted the restaurant's plans. When Flannigan balked about wiring the money to Joe, Joe threatened all kinds of action, things he knew nothing about but hoped he sounded knowledgeable.

"And, Mr. Flannigan, I've started to put two and two together."

"What are you talking about?"

"You, sir, and the restaurant deal that Mr. Banks was working on."

"I don't see that it's any concern of yours, Mr. Huntington. The owner didn't have the proper permits and paperwork to go forward."

"He did, Mr. Flannigan, and you know it. I don't understand why you would want to punish Arthur Banks, a good man, for my quitting at Wysse and Sons. Mr. Wysse and I parted on good terms. And Mr. Banks has been in business in town for twenty years. He's never done a thing to bring this on himself."

"What does any of this business have to do with wiring money for you?"

Joe could practically see him sweating on the other end, and for some reason, he didn't believe Flannigan could be such a rotten egg. Though he hadn't given Joe the loan, he didn't seem to take any pleasure in denying him. Why was he acting like this with Art?

"You will wire the money, sir. It is my money, not yours."

Flannigan conceded defeat and promised the money would be wired immediately. It was a sizable amount and Joe surmised Flannigan didn't want it going to another bank. Or was there more to it than that?

"Mr. Flannigan, as I said before, Mr. Wysse and I parted on good terms. He even included a bonus in my final check, not that it's any of your business, but that's what lets me know he had no hard feelings."

Finally Flannigan murmured, "I may have heard from my nephew that you had left the company stranded. Left them without…I shouldn't say anymore. Joseph, I'll check into the matter. I promise. And I have Charlotte wiring the money."

"I appreciate it, sir. I hope you'll contact Mr. Banks."

Mapes rounded the corner shortly after he finished the call. "The money is being transferred immediately to the First United Bank on Albany. I have a number here that the banker said you would no doubt want as confirmation."

The woman stared at it momentarily and then smiled the first actual smile Joe had seen her make since his arrival. Money did amazing things to some folks. Apparently helped her find her smile. Between her and Flannigan…

If he lived to be a hundred he'd never understand people and money.

"Oh, and I owe you for the call to the bank. Don't want you to think I cheated you." With that, he flipped her a quarter. Her face turned the rosiest red he'd ever seen.

Victoria took a deep breath and did her best to feel awake. Her eyes, heavy as bricks, drooped, trying to pull her back to sleep. "No. I have to talk with Dad and Mom. Surely they'll let me call." She rubbed her eyes and struggled to wake up. Dark outside. How long had she slept?

She smacked lips that felt drier than cotton. Maybe a drink of water would help. She reached for the glass at the side of her bed and greedily gulped the water. Then she swiveled her legs over the edge.

Nurse Malcome walked past the door. "Oh, no, you don't, young lady. Ms. Banks, you must stay in bed."

"But I have to call my parents. They have to know about the surgery in the morning."

Malcome hesitated. "I forgot. Your mother broke her leg, didn't she?"

"A bad break, according to Dad."

"I could call for you. Would that be all right?"

"Oh, please. I'd be grateful. And could you find out how my mother's doing?" With that, she fell back onto the bed. As she lay there, strange thoughts darted through her mind. Joe was part of them. He had held her hand and kissed her fingers. Strange. It all seemed so real. Not like a dream at all, but it had to be. She'd been sleeping all afternoon. Perhaps the medication they'd given her to sleep had caused her to hallucinate. Some medicines did that, right?

It would be nice if it had been Joe, though. She imagined his lips touching her hands, her face… Nonsense. After the way she'd pushed him away, she couldn't expect as much as a kind word. Still, if wishes were real, he'd be sitting right next to her, telling her he loved her more than anything else. And she would do the same. She ran her fingers over her lips. "I love you more than I can say, Joe."

He wouldn't hear her. He'd apparently gone for the day. And who could blame him? Why should he sit with her in the hospital when she didn't have a kind word to say? Even as he'd stepped closer and closer to her at the window. Her heart fluttered a second, and she knew with certainty it had nothing to do with being ill. It had all to do with being very much alive. Fluttering because of how she felt for him. "Oh, Joe. What a mess I've made of things, but I love you enough that I don't want to stick you with a sickly woman for the rest of your life."

She crawled under the sheet and drew the blanket up and over her shoulder. Tomorrow morning would come early and she needed the rest.

Malcome poked her head in. "You still awake?"

"Yes, what did Dad say?"

"Your mother's fine. He said not to worry, but to take care of yourself. Now, let's discuss what's going to happen tomorrow. There are a few things you need to know."

Joe waited outside Victoria's ten-by-ten sterile room and didn't feel the least bit sorry about eavesdropping. He wanted all the details of what would happen to her in the morning, but he figured she wouldn't tell him, if she talked to him at all. This on-again, off-again emotional ride had left him upset enough that here he was, listening in on a conversation.

"I see you out there, Mr. Huntington. You can come in now if you like. I did give Ms. Banks another sedative, but she'll be awake for a while yet. Then in a couple of hours, she'll get more. Helps her to relax, don't you know." She walked out the door and laid a hand on his arm. "Don't stay too long. She needs her sleep. Tomorrow's a big day for her."

He strolled into the room doing his best to appear nonchalant and not as red-faced as he felt for being caught outside the door.

"I thought you'd left for the day." Victoria looked so small and fragile, far from her true self. Her frailty wriggled under his skin and he had to look away momentarily.

He nodded toward the window. "Hey, want me to close the curtains? Sort of cold in here."

"Thank you."

He crossed the room and stopped for a second. "Victoria, listen—"

"Joe, don't say a word. Let me apologize first. I'm so very sorry."

"For what?"

"For *what*? For the terrible way I've treated you since I found out I was ill. For being rude on the train, for acting like a spoiled little girl. If I made a list it would be too long to fit on the stand."

"Why? Why did you do that? I don't understand."

She sucked in her lip and reached over, patted the arm of the chair next to her. "I felt as if we were headed past the point of friendship. Was I wrong?"

"Not really."

"You see?"

"See what? A beautiful woman I care about very much?"

"Joe, it's possible that I could be sitting in a wheelchair the rest of my life, or maybe worse. I didn't want you to be saddled with a broken-down nag or mourning for someone who had become more than a friend. I wanted…I'm not sure what all I wanted, but what I didn't want was for you to be stuck. Maybe harnessed to a woman who wouldn't be able to…" Her face flashed like a red warning light. "Have a family. And I know you want a family. You've said so. Am I right?"

He closed the curtain and slid into the chair beside her. "I *do* want a family. I'd love to have a family, but more than that, I love you, Victoria. I love the way you smile, the way you're full of sass. I like that you don't feel stuck to the image of an everyday woman of the forties. You're independent and dare to be different. I loved that when we played ball as kids. You weren't coy about who you were."

"You what?" Her face brightened and he almost laughed out loud.

"I loved that you wanted to be a professional ball-player. That took courage in a game of mostly boys. One girl playing ball with us boys, two if you count Agatha, but I don't think a two-hundred-pound junior high girl with the build of a linebacker counts." He smiled. "And that type of courage made me want to be around you more. Didn't you notice the guy with the shiner follow-ing you at every possible opportunity?"

"I didn't think you even noticed me unless you had to. Unless Ms. Davies forced you to hold me and waltz."

"I would have paid her to let me hold you. And waltz." He chuckled. "But thankfully, I didn't have to. I guess you don't remember me hiding in the bushes outside school to try and walk you home when you were ten."

"You did what?"

"I thought you might let me carry your books. I hid out three weeks in a row but didn't get up enough gump-tion to step out and ask if you'd let me."

Victoria's bottom lip disappeared between her teeth

and she smiled. "I wish I'd known. I might have treated you differently."

Joe chuckled. "I seriously doubt that. You were only concerned with proving yourself to every boy on the team. And the other teams, as well. No one wanted to bat against you. That arm was legendary in Howell. At least on Walnut Street."

"Well, where does that leave us now? I'm going to allow some doctor I've only met twice to chop a big hole in my chest and do heaven only knows what to try and fix a problem I've apparently had since I was born. I won't be…I won't be whole anymore, Joe. I'll have a huge scar, according to the nurse." Her hand ran down the front of her body. "From here to there and back again. Something he wanted her to be sure to tell me. She admitted it won't be pretty. I'll look like an old broken plate that a kid tried to glue together."

His heart did flips like a jumping Jack. How could he explain that didn't mean anything to him? A scar? So what? "Victoria, I like old plates. My mother had a favorite plate that I hit with a baseball when I was little and—"

"Be serious." She swatted his hand. "It might mean that I'll be…" Her hands covered her face and she started to cry. "Oh, Joe. So many things could go wrong. I don't want you falling in love with me and then—"

"I already have." He reached for her chin and ran his thumb along her jaw, as deliberately as he could. Not wanting to break the contact for a second, he continued to caress her face. "I love you, Victoria, and whatever happens, I'll be here. I'll always be here right beside you." He leaned as close as the chair would allow.

Her eyes drooped a bit as she yawned. "But my

aunt…and uncle." The medication had finally taken effect.

"Your aunt and uncle? What about them and what do they have to do with us?"

"My uncle…took care of her. And chicken for supper."

She yawned wide again, and he pulled his hand away.

"Chicken?" Joe chuckled. "Fried or dumplings?"

"Oh…dumplings. Love Auntie's…dumplings."

Joe smiled. "How about me?"

"You, too. Auntie made the best…oatmeal…raisin, light and fluffy." And with that, she finally dozed off.

Joe had hope, real hope. And he thought he understood why she'd shut him out for so long. He lifted her hand, kissed her fingers for the second time that day and then put her hands under the blanket. It was obvious she hadn't heard a word he said earlier, but it didn't matter now. He'd have all the time in the world to tell her how much he loved her. Adored her. Worshipped the ground she walked on. Over and over again.

Scar or no scar. Did she really think that would matter to him?

With a quick glance around to be sure no one watched, he leaned in and dropped a kiss on her forehead, then her nose and finally on her mouth. So sweet.

Victoria raised an eyelid and smiled. "Love dumplings."

Chapter 13

Art choked on his words as Joe gave him the information on the surgery. "I can't believe what she'll have to—" Joe heard Art clearing his throat. "Do you think I should head out? I mean, I'll have someone come in and stay with Mother overnight. Although I'm pretty sure she'd be mad as a wet hen for leaving her behind, and she's in no condition to make the trip."

"I don't know what you can do if you come, Art."

"Just feels wrong, her being there and us being here. I don't know what I'd do if—"

"You can do plenty. You and the missus can pray. I'm here. There's not a lot left to do. They said she'd be drugged very heavily for some time after. I doubt she'll even realize I'm still here."

"Well, if…if you think so." Art coughed and Joe understood the emotions behind it. Both of her parents wanted to be with her. Joe heard Art sniffle, then cough again. "And one other thing, Joseph. I received a call from a Mrs. Maples today. Very early today."

"Mapes?"

"All right, Mapes. How is it you didn't mention her when *you* called this morning?"

"What…uh. What did she say?"

"She told me about the first amount you paid and then she said something about money you had wired to the bank in Boston. Did I hear her correctly?"

"Art, you just lost the restaurant contract. I thought—"

"So we're going to have the newcomer thinking over the old boss's head? Joseph, we'll discuss this when you return home. Stop worrying about *this* old man, will you? I've made it this far in business. I can survive a little longer. You won't be taking over my financial responsibilities. Not at work, not in my home. Let this be the last said about it."

"Yessir."

"And by the way. I have it on good authority that Wallace Wysse Jr. is in over his head. Apparently he's been making deals with his father's business that aren't all that ethical and the old man didn't like it much when he found out. More than one man in town has complained. I'm thinking the restaurant fiasco is his doing."

"You don't say."

"I do. You wouldn't know anything about that, now, would you?"

"Gotta go, Art. This is costing a lot of money."

"One last thing. A favor?"

"What would that be, Art?"

"If you could give that girl of ours a big hug, we'd appreciate it. If you think she wouldn't mind."

"I don't think she'd mind one bit."

"That's mighty good to hear, son."

Joe left the second floor after thanking the nurses for use of the phone again. They had been so agreeable Joe decided he'd get a bouquet of flowers for them before he took Victoria home.

He wandered through the hospital, praying as he went, but it didn't do the trick. He longed for some peace and quiet to pray. Maybe at the visitors' station they'd be able to tell him where the nearest church was.

"Of course, young fella." An older woman, smiling as though she'd done this job for years and loved helping others, pointed out the door. He followed the line of the thick, arthritic finger and listened to her directions to St. John's. "You go on down. They're happy to have visitors. Or you can pray in our little chapel in the back. Not much, but better than nothing."

"Thanks so much for the help. I think I'll visit the church."

He grabbed a bite and then made his way to the old church at the corner. Stained glass and stone. What looked like a hand-carved wooden door at the front. Appeared as if it had been here long before most of the homes and way before any of the businesses surrounding it.

Joe tried the door. Open...and welcoming. And warm inside as if services were soon expected. It surprised him, but he didn't waste time. He strolled in and took a seat.

"Lord, I'm not exactly sure what to pray, so I'm just going to sit here a bit, and try to feel Your presence. Seems as if I've been away for a while. So much has happened since I came back from the war, and I think I've pushed prayer down my list of things to do. I want more than that from You and for You in my life. But at the moment, I only want to pray for Victoria, not me. She needs a special blessing in the morning, Lord. Please guide the doctor's hands. Keep her safe. Heal her quickly."

"He hears you, son."

Joe, startled and a bit embarrassed for praying aloud, looked up. In a robe and with hair far too long for a modern man, a short wizened fellow held out a hand. "Pastor Roberts, son. And you?"

"Joseph Huntington. From Howell, Michigan, Pastor. I didn't mean to jump, but you were so quiet when you entered."

"I was here. In the front. Praying. Didn't mean to startle you. What brings you here, Joseph? Good name, by the way."

Joe smiled. "A friend is undergoing surgery tomorrow morning. Dr. Gross is actually fixing her heart. I didn't even know doctors could do that."

The pastor tugged at his chin. "Good man."

"You know him?"

"We met at a fundraiser for the children's hospital one year. Fine fellow. Tell me, is your friend smaller than a bread box?"

"Oddly enough, she'd not a child. From what I understand, this isn't common in adults. They usually find it in children. Babies mostly. I don't know how she lived so long with this condition without anyone finding out about it."

"She a quiet, unassuming young lady?"

Unable to stop himself, Joe burst out laughing. "Anything but! She is feisty, tough, gutsy, independent, sometimes downright impossible."

"And?" The pastor's eyebrows rose in a playful manner.

"Beautiful…and just plain wonderful."

"So you love her?" His face hinted that he understood.

Joe let out a loud sigh. "All I wanted when I came back from the war was to start my own business."

"Doing what?"

"Building houses, nice little bungalows for men returning home to start families. I wanted them to have a chance at the dream America gives its people. You know, a chance to make it, have it all if that's possible."

"That's a wonderful dream of yours. What happened to it?"

"Oh, I had a little saved to start with but not enough, and the bank didn't think I was a 'proven' commodity. No loan."

"How did the girl figure in?"

"She didn't. Not at all. A woman wasn't in the plans. All I wanted was the business."

With discernment the pastor chuckled this time. "Women don't usually figure into a man's plans until it's too late for him. So you love this girl. Sort of a surprise to you?"

Joe figured he was completely wearing his heart on his sleeve. "Yes, I'm afraid it was. Well, not really. We've known each other since we were kids. And now she's adamant about my not being hitched to an old nag who's falling apart. I don't feel that way at all. But unless she comes through this operation completely healthy, I doubt she'll have anything to do with me."

"Then let's bow our heads." The man nodded, directing the scene as if in a play. "We have some very important praying to do. Let the Lord have the burden, and we'll take the peace it gives us. How's that sound?"

"Sounds like a plan, Pastor. Because letting her go into surgery tomorrow morning is going to be the hardest thing I've ever done."

Victoria had wanted to stay awake, to continue listening to Joe's voice, but the medicine had won the battle. But now, she just couldn't sleep. The nurse promised she'd be back with more medication. Not to worry. Victoria relaxed against her pillow.

Joe had said something about an old plate. No...she had said that. An old broken plate, but then Joe said he loved antique plates. Even repaired ones. Would he love her after the doctor carved her open like a pumpkin, scraping out—she wasn't sure what all. Dr. Gross had tried to explain to her, but to be honest, she didn't understand exactly what he'd be doing. She just knew if he didn't, she was going to get sicker.

Her fingers grazed her chin where Joe's thumb had run across the skin. The tenderness of his touch lingered, and she longed to have him back—next to her side. Closing her eyes, she imagined him sitting next to her...no, standing with his arms wrapped around her, protecting her from what was about to happen. She fought another yawn.

Oh, how she hated being the helpless female. All of her life she had been the strong one. From baseball to dance classes all the way to running her own studio, Victoria had excelled in so many things. Even classes in school had been easy. And then all of a sudden her health had taken a dive worse than a B-52 on a mission. How had that happened?

Her parents were worrying. Joe, whom she'd had every intention of keeping at a distance, worried also. She had let down her guard, allowed him into her personal life. Not what she'd planned. Her plans had forever allowed her to be in control.

She thought back to their childhood and a particular ball game. It was a very warm day and dry, so all the ballplayers could sweat off the heat as they rounded the bases. Victoria had pitched a particularly strong game; only one run had made it in to the Sluggers' three. And with Joe Huntington knocking dirt from his shoe and up to bat again, there was only one thing left to do to keep her promise to herself.

Victoria pressed her tongue between her lips. She looked to first base where Doggie Hoskins was leading off the plate, then a look to third, out of habit, no one waited to head home. Then her threat to home base. "Heads up, *Master* Huntington."

Joey glanced up in time for his eyes to widen. He couldn't dodge the ball in time. *Thunk!* He took it in the eye and Victoria smiled to herself. "Gotcha."

The umpire, Petey Hoskins, Doggie's older brother, had to call up a pinch runner, because Joe had already headed off the diamond, an old rag covering his face.

Victoria had felt bad once she knew what damage that pitch had done, but still. She'd been the one in control. She had promised herself she'd knock his block off, and she was as good as her word. Horsefeathers! Just a little swelling and a black eye. Buck up and take it, mister. Which was exactly what her father had told her when he found out and sentenced her to two weeks of wood chopping to pay Joe's doctor bill. Joe hadn't said a word, but his mother, who no doubt paid the bill, wasn't quite as generous. She'd accepted the five dollars gladly, and Victoria, blistered hands and all, had slunk away like a dirty skunk.

Now she shook her head, her lips tilting in spite of herself. The fact that Joe spoke to her to this day was amazing. Was he a glutton for punishment? How strange it was to think of being so young…so healthy and strong. But she hadn't been, had she? The heart defect had been there like a monster in the movies, hiding…waiting for its chance to spring out at her. And now, thinking about what the doctors had both told her, the shortness of breath that had been there all along, had been the warning she'd chosen to ignore.

After a short pity party, Victoria chastened herself. If she didn't start flexing her courage like a trained muscle, her life would never be the same.

She sat up in bed, pulled her robe around her shoulders and put a hand over her heart. Before the nurse came in with her last dose of medication, she'd walk down the hall. Look out the window. Appreciate the stars and the heavens. Give the entire situation to God.

I will do well tomorrow. I'm not in control. Not even Dr. Gross is in control. But God is. And if He wants me whole again, I will be. If for some reason I don't come through whole and strong, then I'll have the courage to face even that horrid wheelchair in the corner. God, be with me as You guide Dr. Gross's hands.

Chapter 14

Bits and pieces fluttered through Victoria's mind as she opened her eyes. Her father's laughter. His hand gripping hers like a vise. The single wooden cross on the wall in the chapel. Joe's smile. Early in the morning, Joe had pushed her to the small chapel at the hospital. Had wrapped her in his arms as she clung to him for strength, the cross strong and sure behind them. But that was so long ago.

Now a nurse asked her if she was in pain. Of course she was in pain. But why? When were they going to do the surgery? They had put her out, but if they didn't do the surgery soon, she'd feel every cut. A soft kiss to her forehead. Joe's voice?

Then Phillipe Mandrin was dancing with a dumpling. A dumpling?

Was this all a dream?

Well, she would find out in short order. She tried to sit up. Pressure pushed her back, caused her to catch her breath as the pain ricocheted through her. "Yes! Yes, I'm in pain." Hadn't a nurse just asked her that? "Help!"

A woman in white rushed in. Who was she? A nurse. "Like a little something for your discomfort?"

"If a little is usual...better give me...a lot."

"If it hurts too much to breathe, you can hug a pillow to your chest. Doesn't do much, but it will help some." She headed out of the room.

"They're done? Are they...finished?" Her arms flailed in the air to get the nurse's attention. "Well?"

The nurse returned. "Ms. Banks. Calm down. Yes, they finished two days ago."

"Two days?"

"You've been out. Well, most of it. We've been giving you morphine for the pain. I don't suppose you remember much of anything. You're actually doing quite well."

"I am? I feel...more like that ambulance..."

"What about it?" The nurse lifted a syringe.

"I think...it ran over me. Did you...get the...driver's name?"

The nurse laughed and Victoria tried to smile, but in a few seconds, after the dose of medicine, her eyes felt heavy and pressing once more. The dark shadow, which was all that was left of the nurse, headed for the door.

"She's out again. But you can sit and wait."

Who? Joe? The doctor, maybe. No, he'd be poking and prodding.

She fought to ask, "They did the operation? What happened?"

A comforting voice and blissful sleep.

* * *

Days turned into two weeks and still Victoria's father didn't budge from her side. But it hurt to learn that Joe had left as soon as her father arrived. Why couldn't he have stayed on a couple of days? She wasn't going to bother Dad with questions. He must be missing her mother terribly. No need to add to his misery with her own whining.

Sitting in the chair with a pillow over her chest to help protect her, she did her best Edward G. Robinson. "So, when you gonna break us outta here, Smitty?"

"There's my daughter. That's the girl I've been waiting to see."

"With all these wires and paraphernalia, you didn't think I would have gone anywhere, did you?" She grinned. "Did you talk with Mom this morning?"

At the mention of her mother, Dad's face brightened. If only Victoria could have that kind of loving marriage one day. It seemed unlikely now. According to Dad, Joe had hightailed it out of town as soon as her father arrived. And while she remembered little of it, her father had told her that Joe said to tell her goodbye. Well, maybe hightailed was too strong a word. Her father had simply said Joe left after he arrived.

"I talked to your mother. She's doing very well, sweetie. Even stumping around on crutches to the chagrin of Dr. Cleewell, but you know your mother. Tough as Rosie the Riveter. Told me there were linens to change and launder. I'll bet she's leaning on a crutch to iron the things."

"Dad, Mom would be so embarrassed if she heard you."

"She only acts the part of the delicate rose. Where do you think you got your spunk from?"

Victoria giggled. "Oh, I know where I got it from, thank you. And Auntie played a part in it, as well. There are strong women in both the Banks and White lines."

"You've got me there, sweetheart."

She pulled him toward her for a hug, then winced. "Oooh. Still sore."

He ran a hand through his sparse hair and smiled. "Ah, you women. Really keep a fella on his toes. And now you, with a practically new heart—"

"Dad, I can hardly believe it. Dr. Gross said it all went perfectly. By spring, if all goes well, I'll be teaching dance again. Two more months. Dancing, flying across the floor with my giggling girls."

"He did say no baseball for a while." Her father laughed. "I made sure to ask."

Victoria giggled. "I guess you finally got your way, Dad. Besides, the thought of getting hit in the chest with a ball makes me want to cry." She reached toward the stand next to the bed. "Did you see the card from my girls?" She opened a card with flowers and ballet slippers covering it and all of their names written as neatly as possible.

No card from Joe, though. Not a word from Joe in two weeks.

Joe prayed she would be surprised…in a good way. It was all he could do not to call her and tell her, but if he heard her voice, he would feel compelled to spill the Boston beans. He smiled. Must be getting punchy waiting for her to get home. Where she belonged.

When Art told him he'd received word the roof contract was going through after all, he'd insisted Joe return. He needed someone forceful enough to face down Wallace Wysse Jr. if he tried to use his father's family connections with Mr. Flannigan again. Poor Flannigan. Sure got caught in the middle of a mess trying to remain loyal to his best friend and cousin-in-law, Wallace Wysse Sr.

Sometimes a man got what he deserved. Flannigan admitted to Joe that he'd wanted Joe to work for Wysse to help build the company back up. All his pandering about "prove" yourself to Joe had really been to help the old man bring back his company.

Joe accepted, even respected his honesty this go-round, but Flannigan would have to earn back Joe's trust. That wasn't the way men should do business.

In the meantime, Joe supervised the work site. In his spare time with some of the last of his savings, he worked with two day laborers to get his family's house back in tip-top condition. He'd be bringing a bride home to it soon enough. At least, that was his plan once Victoria returned. He had spoken with Dr. Gross about, well, about their future. Could they get married…have children? And Gross had given him the go-ahead. Hadn't been an easy question to ask, but Joe did. He had to know.

He slapped his hands together, warding off the cold that had finally settled in Howell along with six inches of snow. After an unusually warm December, this cold snap had more bite than a copperhead. But no cold could stop him. This place had to be perfect. All the rooms repainted, the woodwork varnished. The furniture made to look like new, as well.

He walked into the bedroom, gazed at the masterfully crafted light oak and inlaid-wood headboard and dresser. The one new purchase he'd made for them. His parents' old four-poster rope bed had gone into the guest room. But he'd kept the beautiful wedding quilt that had been on his folks' bed as long as Joe remembered. Victoria might not like it, of course, and if she didn't, he would take it off and let her put on whatever she liked. As long as she said yes, she could do as she pleased with the house, with his life, with his heart.

Gerald and Butch Casey put away their tools and headed his way. Gerald thumped him on the back. "I think we're gonna call it a night. Don't touch the paint in the closet. Still wet. And you were right, that light yellow didn't look bad once it dried. Guess I like blue and only blue. Prob'ly why my wife picks out the colors. See you tomorrow night after we get off work at the grain."

Joe nodded. "See you then. You fellas are doing a great job."

Butch raised an eyebrow and laughed. "See that that's reflected in our pay."

No sooner had they left than the phone rang. "Joe here."

"Joe, it's Art. Wanted to let you know we'll be on Thursday's morning train. She's still pretty sore, but Dr. Gross says if all looks well tonight, he'll discharge her late Wednesday."

"When would you leave?" He had to make sure everything was ready before she returned.

"We'll have a good night's sleep at the Shamrock and head out Thursday morning. Thought you should tell Mother. Less than a week and her baby'll be home."

My baby will be home. But Joe didn't say that. She

might… No, he refused to think she wouldn't say yes. "I'll let her know, sir. Safe trip. We'll see you both Saturday."

He walked back into the bedroom and snatched the small velvet box out of the dresser. When he opened the lid, a sparkler met his gaze. His grandmother's ring. Then his mother's. Would she want a secondhand ring, a two-time hand-me-down? He'd taken it to the jeweler in town and had the man clean it up. A large daisy-cut diamond in the center, with smaller diamonds on each side shone bright as the sun. This must have cost his grandfather plenty in his day, but then, Gramps had been a very wealthy man.

Before he could finish dialing the Bankses' number so he could talk to her mother, Joe stopped and put the phone back in the cradle. He really wanted to call Victoria, but with another quick glance at the ring, he couldn't. No, he had to keep all the news to himself for a few more days. He had to wait until she returned. Then he'd show her the house, get down on one knee and ask her to marry him. So no phone call. He didn't exactly keep secrets all that well.

With his mission back on track, he called Mrs. Banks, then picked up his tools. There was still his parents' antique dining room table to refinish.

Chapter 15

Victoria barely swallowed her food. Her father had bought her a chicken sandwich and milk. Yes, he still saw her as thirteen years old. Oh, well, he'd probably always see her that way, and he'd been overly protective since her surgery.

Another quick bite and she passed the rest of the sandwich to him to finish. "I've had enough, Dad. But I am getting my appetite back. I can't wait to get back home and make a pie. A custard pie. Oooh, that sounds so good after all that terrible hospital food."

"They certainly charged enough for it." He blushed immediately. "I'm sorry. I didn't mean to say that."

"Oh, Dad. Are we going to be able to afford that huge bill?"

"You don't know?"

"Know what?"

He shifted in his seat and faced her. "Joe paid over

half of that bill. I'll be sending them the rest over the next four months."

"Joe? He paid my bill?"

"They wouldn't go ahead with the surgery unless half of the estimate was paid. He didn't tell you?"

Victoria's mind drifted to the times he had started to share things with her but she'd cut him off, complained or whined. Or the times he'd sat there as she drifted in and out of sleep. Poor Joe. Not only had he been stuck with her, but he'd paid part of her bill.

"Why did he do that, Dad?"

"He was afraid my business was suffering too much, and he didn't want me worrying with Mother laid up. He's a fine one, that boy."

That man was hardly a boy, but she wouldn't say that to her father. Besides, chances were, he truly had done it as a favor to her father. In spite of all he'd said to her, he had not called even once. No letter, not a note. Surely if he had real feelings for her he would have at least scribbled a note that said *get well*.

"Sure, Dad. Salt of the earth. I intend to pay him back."

"Of course. With the roofing contract I can reimburse him once we're home."

"Oh. All right. Then I'll repay you when the time comes."

Her dad shot her a glance, a wary expression that asked her questions she had no intention of answering.

Joe held Mrs. Banks's arm to keep her steady in the snow as she leaned forward on the crutches. She had refused to stay in the auto and wait where it was warm. "I'm not ready to roll over and die yet, Joseph." She dug the crutches firmly into the snow. "It will take more than a couple of inches of snow to keep me down."

"Ma'am, I never thought—"

"Don't you mind what you thought." Then she smiled and patted his cheek. She was still a lovely lady, and Joe pictured Victoria in twenty years. "Thank you, Joseph. You're a dear boy. Have I told you how much I appreciate all you've done?"

He settled against the side of the platform, hat in hand, and nodded. He chuckled, wondering why he'd bothered to bring the hat along. He glanced over the open track, plopped it back on his head and heaved a sigh. Tucking the scarf his brother's family had given him deeper into his overcoat, he shivered against the chilly air.

"You all right, Joseph?"

"Fine, ma'am. Anxious is all. And cold."

"So am I. From the moment we discovered our baby would be having heart surgery and I broke my leg, I've been stuck at home. Nothing to do but worry. Unable to be with her at a time like this, when a girl needs her mom most, made me a little stir-crazy. Yes, Joseph, I'm very anxious to see my daughter." She smiled. "And you're right. It is cold today."

A long low whistle sounded in the distance. Joe stood tall, searched the horizon. Nothing yet. He checked his watch. It wouldn't be long now.

Ten minutes later the train pulled into the station amid steamy soot that fell in clouds of white. Mrs. Banks inched forward, but Joe stayed back, allowing her the time with her daughter and husband. "Be careful, ma'am."

"Oh, fiddlesticks. I'm downright talented with these things." She grinned and held one of the crutches aloft like a trophy.

Like every month since the war had ended, the train was full of servicemen returning home. It would be months until everyone was home. Khaki-green and hopeful faces rushed through the mist, grabbed duffels and headed toward open arms.

Mrs. Banks burst into tears as Art did his best to support both women. Joe noticed Victoria's wobbly steps. "Joe, if you'll take my two girls, I'll get the suitcases."

Mrs. Banks sniffled and dabbed at her eyes. "I'm staying right next to you, dear. You've been gone too long. Grab on tighter so I can go with you." She clutched at Art's arm.

"You," Art said, "will climb into the auto and get off that leg." He pecked her cheek and left to retrieve the suitcases. He held up a hand. "No arguments, my dear. I want you safe first and foremost."

"Here, Joseph." She pushed Victoria toward Joe. "I think you two have things to discuss."

Joe cupped Victoria's elbows, steadying her. "Seemed like you couldn't get here fast enough for me. We've been waiting over an hour."

Her nose tilted. Classic slugger pose. "And why would you care when I got home?"

"What?" His fingers tightened on her arms. "Victoria. I've been going crazy when I couldn't be with you. I hated leaving. Art had to practically shove me on the train. But he—"

"He what, Joe? Don't bring my poor father into this. I was given medication to knock me out and you were gone. Just like that." She snapped her fingers through gloves and it didn't make much of a point. But he knew better than to laugh. "No goodbye, no calls, no notes. What did that mean? I can tell you. It meant you didn't care one bit." Her attitude only doubled and he could almost picture her on the mound.

"I—uh. You see…"

"Uh-huh. You told me what you thought I wanted to hear so that I'd do well with the operation. Didn't want the poor girl facing life and death without something to look forward to. After that, no need to continue leading me on. I get it, Joe. No one has to beat me over the head. I appreciate the kindness. Now let's go on about our business. You to your home and me to mine."

"Hmm. Beat you over the head. Like a caveman?"

"What does that mean?"

"You are so impossible." Without a thought to what anyone else might think, Joe pulled his hands off her arms, then reached around and wrapped her securely in his grasp. He held tight, leaving no chance for her to escape, then leaned toward her, their breath a dance of fog before his eyes. "It means I love you, Victoria Banks. I didn't call, didn't write, because if I had, I would have given in and told you what I was doing."

She bit her lip the way that said she was unsure what to say next. Then Joe's gaze narrowed on her lips until she stopped, looked away. "Wh-what do you mean… what you were doing? Just what *have* you been doing?"

"I have a surprise for you later this week. Not today. Today you need to go home and rest. Have the meal Mrs. Evans cooked for everyone. And I have to talk with your father."

She twirled a piece of hair and tucked it behind her ear in a hesitant manner. "I thought you talked with him almost every day…about business. That's what he said. Questions about the restaurant roof and the contract."

Joe kissed the tip of her nose. Chilly response. "I did fill him in on those details. But not only that. I was checking on you. Making sure you were all right. It was killing me not to talk with you, but you see, I'm not good at keeping secrets."

"Secrets, oh, sure." She struggled against his hold, the moment of uncertainty long gone.

"Yes. Secrets. Why are you fighting me so hard?"

She let out a rush of air. "I'm not good at this *he loves me, he loves me not* business."

"He loves you."

Victoria stopped struggling. Her eyes widened and some of the attitude withered. "He does?"

"More than anything…more than anyone…ever."

"Really?" Her face tilted up. If it had been anyone other than Victoria, he would have sworn she was almost begging him to kiss her.

"That's right. I love you enough to have secrets."

"Then I guess I can't wait to find out what you've done, Joe." Without warning, she snuggled into his embrace. "How about a hint what this is all about?" She licked her lips.

No more wasting time. He'd give her a hint, all right. With that, Joe bent down and captured her lips. The time in Lansing when he had returned home to no arms, no lips…well, he made up for it this time. This meeting in a train station had "welcome" spelled out in huge letters, and he, by everything he loved, wouldn't miss the chance.

This time when Victoria's heart galloped like a mare, she didn't worry, well, not much. At first that old feeling returned, and then she realized this only meant her heart appreciated what her lips were doing.

She grinned up at him. "I think I'm all wobbly again."

Joe immediately pulled back, a worried expression on his face. "Are you all right?"

"I'm just fine. For some reason, my legs feel like Grandma's jelly. You'd better hold me tighter."

"I aim to please, ma'am." He slipped his hands under her open coat and around her waist so close it was hard for her to breathe. But she didn't complain; rather, she snuggled into the warmth of his hold.

Locked in to his gaze, she put gloved hands on either side of his face and pulled him down into her embrace. And this time, she didn't wait for Joe to initiate the kissing. *He likes my independent spirit? Well, here goes.*

That kiss sealed everything Victoria had ever wanted. Baseball, dance, nothing lived up to the touch of Joe's gentle lips on hers, a kiss that promised a future, a life filled with his tender love. Once they finally came back up for air, she nodded. "I've actually never been better, Joe. Dr. Gross even said so." Was that her eyes she saw reflected in his? They looked like thousands of little diamonds...stars in a brilliant sky. "And now that I've plied you with kisses, how about those surprises?"

"Oh, no, you don't, missy." He nipped the edge of her lip. "I think we'd better bargain some more."

Epilogue

Eighteen months later

Joe, sweaty from the summer sun and hours of work with Art, ambled into the house…their house. The house he had completely remodeled top to bottom as a surprise for Victoria before they were married.

Victoria's handiwork showed in every corner of the property. Roses in big washtubs filled the front porch. Orange-blossom bushes edged the drive, and irises filled the yard. Maybe most men didn't notice such things, but Joe did. She had taken such pride in the house.

He stopped daydreaming and dashed for the front door.

He stopped at the threshold, and stared as his gorgeous wife, with four-month-old Lindy wrapped to her mother's back papoose-style, danced around the front room. Victoria's arms in the air, she stretched and bobbed, her feet delicate and sure with each step. Her voice shouted out the words to "Doin' What Comes Natur'lly."

And she was. Dancing was as natural to Victoria as breathing was to Joe. He respected that. He also respected the fact that Victoria had already bought a softball and tiny toy baseball mitt for their little princess. Ah, yes. Life would never be boring married to the most beautiful girl who ever lived. And, oh, Victoria did know how to live life.

He slipped in behind her and dropped a peck on Lindy's pudgy pink cheek. "Glabba, gibbe, gooby." Her little arms waved in the air, a conductor to her mother's symphony of song.

Victoria spun around on her toes. "How long have you been standing there?"

"Long enough to fall in love with the two sweetest girls in the world." He leaned down and pecked Victoria on the lips, then drew her into his arms and waltzed the two of them around the room. Lindy giggled and cooed.

"Oh, no, mister. You don't get off so easily as that." She drew on her attitude once again. "A peck on the lips? Can't you do better than that when I have such a fabulous surprise for you?"

Pie. Apple pie, he was sure.

"But I'm all dirty and sweaty."

"And handsome and wonderful and—"

"Oh, yeah." Joe crushed her to him, doing a better job of capturing her lips. "And I am so blessed, Mrs. Huntington, to have you in my life." He leaned over her shoulder and tweaked Lindy's little nose. "With the next pitcher for the Walnut Sluggers there, I don't know how our lives could get any better."

She lifted her hand, the dainty ring sparkling like

fire on her finger. Then Joe noticed her face sparkled, as well.

"What would you say to a boy?"

"Really?"

She nodded. "Hopefully it will be a boy."

His heart soared. Kissing her...hard this time. "I'd say this go-round, we'd better get a bat...and maybe some bandages for his eye."

* * * * *